TO ZOE AND SAGE, WITH LOVE

Chapter One

The oddest thing about Angelina D'Angelo was that no one could remember a time when she didn't live in Willow Falls. The oldest man in town, Bucky Whitehead, swears Angelina was an old lady when HE was a boy. But when questioned, Angelina just smiled. The person asking would get so distracted by watching the duck-shaped birthmark wiggle on her cheek, they would forget their question altogether.

Angelina, small and swift, was moving even faster than usual because today was the day she had been waiting for. She had been waiting a LONG time. Her volunteer badge securely fastened to her hip pocket, she whooshed down the hall of the Willow Falls Birthing Centre and stopped short in front of the nursery window.

1

Pressing her hands against the cool glass, she searched the faces of the newborn babies until she found the two she was looking for.

First, the boy. Pink cheeks, a mop of black hair, clenched fists. And then, in the next bassinet, the girl. A thin coating of blond fuzz on her head, a sweet smile on her lips. Angelina knew it was just gas, but that smile told her a lot. It told her all she needed to know. She stepped back and waited. A few minutes later, the two mothers appeared from different directions, wheeled up to the window by their happily exhausted husbands. The younger of the two women had her dark curly hair pulled into a loose ponytail. The other, a blonde with a fashionable bob, had already changed out of her hospital gown into a running suit. The men nodded a polite hello to each other.

No one noticed Angelina. She had perfected the art of blending into the background.

"Which one's yours?" the dark-haired woman asked.

"That one," the blonde said, pointing to the little girl who was rubbing her closed eyes. "She's our second. We have a two-year-old at home."

The other woman smiled. "She's precious."

Then she pointed to the boy who was now happily sucking his fist. "That one's ours. He's our first. But we want lots more kids, right, honey?" She reached up for her husband's hand and squeezed it.

"Let's see how this one goes," he said, laughing kindly.

A soft, strong voice from behind them asked, "What have you decided to name them?"

The four craned their necks around, surprised to see Angelina. They had thought they were alone in the hallway.

The boy's mother replied, "Leo. After my husband's great-grandfather, Leonard Fitzpatrick."

The girl's mother said, "That's funny, we're naming Amanda after my husband's great-grand*mother*, Amanda Ellerby."

The men were suddenly struck with an uneasy feeling, like they were remembering something out of a storybook someone read to them when they were children. But the old woman was talking again, so they shook off the feeling.

"Being born on the same day is very special. I believe Amanda and Leo will be the best of friends." She said this very confidently. "You will be sure to celebrate this day together every year, no? The day of their birth?"

"Um, sure," the mothers promised, smiling graciously at each other. Neither really meant it.

"A very wise decision," Angelina said with a quick nod. "Blessings to all of you."

A moment later she whooshed back down the hall and out of sight.

"That was strange," said Amanda's father.

"Angelina's an odd one," said Leo's father. "But I'm sure you know that. She's lived in Willow Falls for ever."

Amanda's parents shook their heads. "We just moved to town a few months ago," her mom said.

"My family used to live here," Amanda's dad added, "but my parents moved away before I was born. We really don't know anyone."

So Leo's parents told them the important things, like where to find the best pizza, who offered the best prices on diapers. And when they parted, neither expected to see the other again.

They were wrong.

Chapter Two

10 YEARS AGO — MR MCALLISTER'S MAGIC CASTLE BIRTHDAY PARTY PALACE

Amanda crawled over to the inflatable white castle that took up half the room and poked it with her finger. She giggled and poked it again. She liked it here. The air smelled like cake. She looked around for her parents. Her father was lifting her older sister, Kylie, on to a big, stuffed pony. Her mother was talking to the man behind the counter, who wore a funny floppy hat.

"What do you mean we have to share the birthday room?" Amanda's mother said. "Please check again. I booked my daughter's party months ago."

The man shook his head. "I'm sorry, ma'am. Mistakes happen. The room is plenty big enough to share. You probably won't even notice the other party."

Amanda's mother sighed and drummed her manicured nails on the counter. "Fine. Who's the other party?"

The man pointed towards the door, which was swinging open with a jingle of bells. "Here they come now."

A dark-haired woman in a long skirt strolled through the door. The little boy perched on her hip clutched a purple bear. Amanda tilted her head to see both the boy and the bear better. The boy squirmed, and his mother set him down on the floor while she went up to the counter.

Amanda's mother's eyebrows arched in surprise. "*You?*"

"You?" the boy's mother echoed, recognition glimmering in her eyes.

Then they laughed.

"Is that Leo?" Amanda's mother asked, pointing at the little boy who was now crawling towards the castle.

The other woman nodded and then searched the room until she found Amanda. "And that lovely little girl must be Amanda."

Amanda's mother nodded. They looked back at each other and laughed again. "I guess we're celebrating their birthday together after all!" Leo's mother said, grinning widely.

"Sure looks like it," said Amanda's.

As Leo crawled towards Amanda, he dragged his bear on the ground. Amanda watched, curious. Her mother would never let her bring her teddy out in public. Too many germs. Not that Amanda knew what germs were, only that they were bad to put in your mouth.

When Leo reached the castle they stared at each other. Amanda was used to being around other babies at the park and during storytime at the library. But she usually stayed far away from them. Leo felt different somehow. She reached out and tugged on one of the boy's curls. He laughed and handed her his bear. As a younger sister, Amanda wasn't used to people simply handing over their toys. She took it, but cautiously. They sat there, watching each other, until their mothers came over and started fussing over them. It wasn't until later, after cake had been eaten and songs sang, that the two of them were able to escape. They crawled towards each other, and then with some unspoken understanding, both pushed off the floor with their hands and stood. Four parents and many bemused party guests watched as the two babies took their very first steps, crashed into each other, and fell to the floor laughing.

Outside, a small old woman approached the glass window. Behind the counter, Mr McAllister of the Magic Castle Birthday Party Palace turned and winked at her. She gave a quick, satisfied nod and whooshed away. Yes, everything was going exactly according to plan.

Chapter Three

"But what if I land on my head?" I ask. "And then, you know, all the other body parts?' An image fills my head of broken bones and scraped knees for my party tomorrow. "Maybe I shouldn't do this."

"You won't fall this time," promises Stephanie. "You need to get this move down before tryouts tomorrow. C'mon, I'm your best friend. I wouldn't let you fall."

"If you were really my best friend," I say with a pout, "you wouldn't make me try out at all." I'm stalling and she knows it. What I really want to say is, *if you're my best friend you'd tell me to try out for the marching band instead.* But we both know that would never happen. Besides the fact that marching band is considered uncool, I've

9

never played my drums anywhere other than my own basement.

"C'mon, Amanda. I keep telling you. If we want to hang out with Mena and Heather and Jess, we need to be on the team. And to be on the team you need to be able to do a back handspring. *Without* falling."

I stare across my backyard, willing my mom to come out and tell us it's getting late and Stephanie has to go home. But she's not back from work yet. I can't count on Dad, either. He's inside cleaning up from our usual mom-working-late dinner – macaroni and cheese with salami melted on top. Even if he was out here, he'd see my frantic look and just smile and wave. Dad's a good guy. He just doesn't pick up on a lot of things. Kylie is my only hope, which means I'm doomed. She and a preppy boy named Dustin from her science class are on the back porch trying to turn lead into gold or some other sciency thing for their final project of the year. Kylie's twirling her long blond hair around her finger, which is her way of flirting, but Dustin doesn't seem to notice. He's the breed of boy whose clothes actually match, and whose hair looks like it was professionally cut in a salon. He doesn't look like he's climbed a tree or built a fort in his entire life. In an alternate universe where my older sister actually paid any sort of attention to me, she might see that I'm scared and come to my rescue. Alas, this is not an alternate universe and she's more interested in him than me.

I stall some more. "What if I don't want to be friends with Mena and Heather and Jess?"

Stephanie shakes her head, unwilling to even answer. I sigh. OK, she's got me. Of course I want to be friends with them. They're the most popular girls in the fifth grade. And if we make the team, our status in sixth grade will be secure.

Out of ideas, I point to my midsection. "I think my centre of gravity is too low. It might be physically impossible for me to do a back handspring."

Stephanie tilts her head at me. "Your what is what?"

I open my mouth to explain, but she waves it away. "Don't make me count to three. At three I go over and tell Kylie you stole her favourite red sweater last winter and left it on the school bus."

"OK, OK!" With a final glance behind me to make sure the mat is in place, I take a deep breath, raise my arms next to my head, then swing them down really fast. Bending my knees, I spring backwards before I can change my mind. In a panic, I try to remember what Stephanie taught me. Lean back, tighten abs, keep arms locked, look for a place to land my hands. But time seems to accelerate faster than its normal speed and before I know it, I'm crumpled in a heap, the freshly mown grass tickling the back of my neck. Somehow I'm a good two feet away from the mat. Dazed, I stare up at the dusky sky. "How'd I do?"

Stephanie sits down next to me, tucking her legs underneath her. "Well, you didn't break anything, so there's that."

"OK, girls," my mother calls from the back door, waving us inside. "Time to call it a night. Amanda, you need to come set up for the party."

Sure, *now* she saves me. Couldn't she have come home five minutes earlier? Stephanie helps me up, and I dust the dirt and grass off my clothes. I have one more day to get this back handspring down. It doesn't look promising, but I really don't want to disappoint Stephanie. This last year would have been so much harder if it hadn't been for her. We walk around the side of the house to the driveway, where she left her bike propped against the fence.

"I'll keep working on it tonight," I say as she straps on her helmet. "I promise."

She gives me a look that says she's unconvinced. "Why don't you ask Kylie to spot you?"

I shake my head, frowning. "She's too busy trying to get her science partner to ask her to the Seventh Grade Fling. I don't think she's having any luck, though."

"You wouldn't think someone as pretty as your sister would have any trouble getting a guy."

I wouldn't have thought so, either. People say Kylie and I look a lot alike, but unless I have a major growth spurt, my hair suddenly becomes soft and silky, and my freckles miraculously disappear, I won't look anything like her when I get to be thirteen.

"Didn't that guy Jonathan already ask her? From down the street?"

"Yeah, but no way would she go with him. He still plays with LEGOs."

"Yikes," Stephanie says, swinging her leg over her seat. "That would bring your sister down, like, five rungs on the coolness ladder. See you tomorrow. Happy early birthday!"

She pedals off down the driveway. I call after her, "There's a coolness ladder?"

She just waves and calls over her shoulder, "Don't forget to practise!"

I sigh. I wonder if practising in my head counts. I can easily picture myself doing a perfect routine. Somehow it comes out differently once gravity gets involved.

Not wanting to walk by Kylie and Mr Every Hair in Place, I go through the front door instead. Mom's overflowing briefcase is leaning against the bottom of the stairs, and I barely avoid tripping over it. Ever since she got promoted to account executive, her briefcase is getting bigger and bigger, and her time at home is getting shorter and shorter. I know she has to work, but I'm pretty tired of mac 'n' cheese and salami.

"There you are, Amanda," she says, coming around the corner from the kitchen. She's still wearing her work clothes. Today it's a grey business suit. She's holding a tape dispenser in one hand, and a thick roll of red crepe paper in the other. She thrusts the paper at me. "Look what I found for the Red Carpet. Isn't it perfect?"

I muster up a smile that I don't feel. Why did I agree to a Hollywood movie theme?

"Your father already hung the movie posters and sprinkled the gold stars everywhere, so once we lay down the carpet, all we have to do is put out the paper plates and cups, and blow up the balloons."

I follow her down the stairs to the basement where she picks up the stack of RSVPs that have come back.

"Looks like about fifteen kids are coming," she says, fanning them out in her hands. "That's a very respectable number."

She means that's a very respectable number considering I'm not the only person in school having their birthday party tomorrow. One of the cards catches my eye. I pull it from the pile and hold it up to her.

"Did you mail Leo an invitation?" I ask accusingly.

She leans over to straighten the *Freaky Friday* poster that has started to slip down the wall.

"Mom?"

"OK, yes, I invited him. How could I not?"

I grit my teeth. "Don't you remember what he did to me last year?"

"Of course I do, honey, but maybe, well, maybe you overreacted a bit?"

I debate either bursting into tears or screaming, neither of which are likely to make me feel better, and one of which could get me grounded. I count to ten inside my head, then crumple the RSVP and toss it in the trash can. "Let's just set up for the party, OK?"

Mom nods. "I hope you'll still try to enjoy your birthday," she says, bending down to unroll the red paper. "After all, you only turn eleven once."

"Thank God," I mutter.

. . . .

When the basement looks as "Hollywood" as it's going to get, I head up to my room. Lying neatly across my bed is the costume Mom picked up for me since she didn't have time to make one. Apparently Halloween costumes are scarce in June because I'm now staring at a blue-and-white dress, red sparkly shoes, and a wicker picnic basket. I'm Dorothy from *The Wizard of Oz*. I shiver involuntarily. *The Wizard of Oz* has always given me the creeps. All those flying monkeys. Why couldn't I be someone like Fiona from the *Shrek* movies, or better yet, that girl from the *Fantastic Four* who can turn invisible? If I were invisible, no one would see me duck out of my own party.

16

I toss the dress over my desk chair and find myself staring at the bottom drawer. The one that's been locked for a year. Inside is only one thing – my birthday party photo album. Each year Mom puts one picture in there. I used to love looking at them, but after last year I locked it away. It was just too hard seeing it on my shelf every day. I open the top desk drawer and fish around in the back. I find the small silver key and turn it over in my hand. Before I can think better of it, I unlock the drawer, pull out the album and plop down on the bed. I run my hands over the yellow cover with the picture of a smiling pastel green frog on it. I don't know why my mom picked out this frog album, instead of one with oh, anything else on it.

Here goes nothing.

1st Birthday: I flip open the cover, and can't help but smile. There we are, propped up in front of a white inflatable castle. Leo with all his curls (he cuts them off now), and me in my pink party dress, sucking my thumb. It's hard to believe that if the birthday palace hadn't been double-booked, Leo and I wouldn't have celebrated our next ten birthdays together. I used to think we were so lucky, but after what happened last year, I'm not so sure.

2nd Birthday: Leo is holding a tambourine, and his arm is a blur as he brings it down on his hip. I'm holding two drumsticks and smiling madly. Even back then I loved the drums. Dad told me they kept handing me other instruments at our Musical Babies party, but I wouldn't let go of those sticks.

3rd Birthday: Leo and I are kneeling on either side of a baby goat, our hands resting on its back. This day is one of my earliest memories. One of the baby bunnies went missing, and I cried, but then Leo found it curled up asleep inside a blue plastic ice-cream bowl. Later he wrote his first poem about it. I once heard Mom call his parents "overgrown hippies" because they grow their own vegetables and encourage their son to write poetry.

4th Birthday: Marvin the Magnificent is pulling a magic wand out of Leo's ear. Leo's mouth is frozen in a "wow". I'm next to him, clapping and staring. Right before Leo's mom cut our cake, a dove flew out of Marvin's top hat. I can recognize most of the guests in the photo. Willow Falls is such a small town that the same kids came to our parties each year. Now, of course, that's all changing.

5th Birthday: Leo is smiling and holding up a hand-painted flowerpot. My face is starting to crumple because I don't like the way mine turned out. The woman who owned the Creative Kids Pottery Studio hadn't yet filled them with dirt or the little seed that I was sure would never grow. But the seed *did* grow. It thrived, in fact, for another five years until the night of my tenth birthday. I quickly turn the page.

6th Birthday: Bowling! Leo and I proudly hold up our balls. Mine is pink, his is green. They can't weigh much more than beach balls. Behind us I can see those bumpers that they stuck in the lanes so we never got gutter balls. Stephanie had moved to town the month before, so this was her first appearance at our party. From then on, the three of us did everything together.

7th Birthday: Gymnastics, of all things! Leo and I are hanging off the balance beam, pretending we're falling. Back then I was actually pretty good at that stuff. Together the two of us were fearless – swinging around the uneven bars, jumping up on to the horse-thingy, and flying off. In the background of the picture I can see Stephanie and Ruby Gordon with their arms up, ready to do backflips. If I didn't need so much help now, Stephanie would have been practising with Ruby tonight, instead of me.

8th Birthday: Disco party! I'm wearing a big multicoloured wig, and Leo has on mirrored sunglasses and a rainbow headband. According to our parents, this is how people dressed in the seventies. We're on the dance floor of the Willow Falls Community Centre party room, boogying to the beat of KC and the Sunshine Band.

9th Birthday: The beach! It was warm that year for the beginning of June so our parents took us all to the beach, about an hour away. The picture shows me and Stephanie burying Leo up to his neck in the sand. He's really lying down, but it looks like he's standing up. He's wearing that corny beach hat of his that says "Keep On Keeping On".

I don't need to turn the page to know there isn't a photo of our tenth birthday.

Our party was held at Leo's house. His mom had decorated it like the Haunted Mansion at Disneyland. She set up this whole spooky maze through the house where you had to use hidden clues to find your way out. Before going through it I ran upstairs to use the bathroom. When I passed Leo's room I heard him in there with a bunch of his guy friends. I stopped when I heard my name, and pressed up against the wall to listen.

"Yeah, why do you still have your party with a girl, man?" Vinnie Prinz asked. "It's really lame."

I held my breath.

Leo said, "Yeah, I know it's stupid. My mom makes me."

Another boy chimed in. "Can't you just tell her you don't want to? I mean, dude, it's *your* birthday."

Normally I'd have rolled my eyes at "man" and "dude", but I was too shocked.

"Nah," Leo said, his voice flat. "Plus, I wouldn't want Amanda to get all upset. She doesn't, you know, have that many other friends."

That was all I needed to hear. I ran downstairs and out the door so fast that at first, no one knew I'd left. My parents found me crying on our front steps. That night I took everything that reminded me of Leo out of my room. The hand-painted flowerpot was the first to go. Out the window, in fact. I heard it crash into the bushes below. Then I gathered up all the sweatshirts I'd borrowed, the mix CDs he had burned for me, the comic books he gave me because he joked that the superheroes looked like the two of us, and put them all in a box which I pushed out to the hall. I was about to throw the photo album out the window, too, but my mom came in at that point and convinced me to lock it away instead.

Leo didn't know at first why I had left or why I was so upset. My mom eventually told his mother what I'd heard. I haven't spoken one word to him since that night.

Feeling even worse now after that trip down memory lane, I close the album and place it back in the drawer. Maybe I'll look at it again in another eleven years. Maybe by then it won't hurt so much.

I throw on my pyjamas and head to the bathroom to brush my teeth. I pass Kylie's room and hear her on the phone. Her voice sounds sort of choked up. But when she comes out of the room she just breezes by me and flips her hair like she doesn't have a care in the world.

After the fastest teeth brushing in history, I turn off the light and climb into bed without even reading first. In a few hours I'm going to be eleven. That's a whole new decade. I stare up at the flowers Mom and I painted on my ceiling a few years ago. The moonlight illuminates them, and they make me smile. I have fifteen kids coming here tomorrow night. That's fifteen friends who chose to come to my party instead of Leo's. Even if I'll be stuck wearing a Dorothy costume, I'm going to try to have a good time. After all, like Mom said, I'm only going to turn eleven once.

I just wish I wasn't doing it alone.

Chapter Four

I reach out to turn off my alarm, open my eyes, and scream! Someone's standing in the middle of my room. He's short and squat, and his arms and legs are waving wildly. It's too dark to see anything clearly. Safety tips run through my head. *Stop, drop, and roll?* That doesn't seem helpful. *Duck and cover?* That one's better. I throw the covers over my head and lie still. Why isn't the intruder saying anything? After a few heart-pounding minutes, I force myself to peek out from the top of the blanket. With one swift move, I flick on my lamp.

Huh. OK, so it's not a person. It's a SpongeBob SquarePants happy birthday balloon with streamers for arms and legs. My parents must have snuck him in while I was sleeping. That's a heck of a thing to do to someone!

Once my heart rate returns to normal, I throw on jeans, my favourite red T-shirt, and the beaded necklace I made at Stephanie's birthday party a few months ago. I run a comb through my thick hair, which only makes it more poofy. I look like I'm wearing a helmet.

Everyone knows that teeth brushing and face washing are things that birthday girls don't have to do, so my bathroom routine is very fast today. I step into the hall and am surprised to find Kylie's door wide open. It's always closed and locked, whether she's in there or not. She must have left it open by mistake when she went to run. No one was more surprised than me when she suddenly took up running first thing in the mornings. This was the same girl who used to make me sign Mom's name to her "get-out-of-gym" slips because she hated breaking a sweat. I glance around to make sure she's not about to run up the stairs, and then stick my head into her room. It looks like a tornado swept through it. Clothes are everywhere. I can't imagine how she finds anything. But the most interesting thing is the purple notebook on the floor by the bed. The one marked KYLIE'S DIARY: KEEP OUT OR SUFFER THE CONSEQUENCES.

I certainly don't want to suffer any consequences, so I hurry on down the stairs. After all, what could it say that would be interesting? Kylie's life is so perfect. Her biggest fear is chipping a nail before homeroom and not having the right colour polish to fix it.

Dad is the only one in the kitchen when I arrive. Unshaven and in his pyjamas, he gives me a raspy hello as he pours himself some tea from the teapot. My dad doesn't drink tea. Unless he's sick. Oh no!

"Dad! You can't be sick. My party's tonight. You're the DJ!"

He sneezes twice in a row and then says, "I'll be fine, honey. Happy . . . achoo . . . birthday . . . achoo! Don't you worry about . . . about . . . achoo!!"

I cover my mouth and nose. The last thing I want is to get sick today. My mother rushes into the room, fully dressed and made up. She has a big presentation today at the ad agency where she works. I heard her practising her speech when I was trying to fall asleep.

"Happy birthday, sweetie!" She leans over to kiss my forehead. She gets my hair instead. "Feel any older?"

I consider her question as I pour milk on my Corn Pops. "I think I'm growing. My feet were closer to the edge of the bed this morning. Thanks for the balloon, by the way."

Dad chuckles. It dissolves into a wheeze. When he collects himself he says, "You liked that, eh? And your sister said you were too old for SpongeBob."

"I *am* too old, but it's still cute. Especially, you know, when it wasn't trying to attack me."

"Hmm?" he says, opening the morning newspaper.

"Nothing," I say, quickly shovelling cereal into my mouth.

"I've gotta run," Mom says, sticking a granola bar in the pocket of her blazer. "I'll be home early to help you get ready."

I nod. Images of that uncomfortable-looking Dorothy costume flit across my mind.

Mom kisses my head again, waves to Dad from a safe distance germwise, and strides out of the room.

Mom usually takes us on her way to work, except when she leaves early like this. I turn to Dad. "I guess you're not going to drive us to school?"

He shakes his head. "I'm sorry." He sneezes again, just to prove he's really sick. "You'll just have to take the bus today."

Ugh. The bus. Kylie and I are lucky, we only wind up taking the bus a few times a month. It's smelly and loud and my shoes always stick to the floor.

I hurry to finish my cereal since the bus comes in five minutes. Kylie runs in, grunts hello to Dad, grabs her lunch bag from the fridge, and runs out the door. No good mornings. No happy birthdays.

"She means well," Dad says.

"No she doesn't," I reply.

He laughs, and then starts hacking up a lung.

Ducking out of the way of flying sick-person germs, I grab my heavy backpack and run out after Kylie. I'm halfway to the stop before I realize I forgot my lunch. I check my watch. The bus was due three minutes ago, so it's already late. Can I risk it? The bus rounds the corner, answering my question.

Lunchless and out of breath, I climb on behind Kylie. She passes right by her science partner, Dustin, without saying anything. Maybe it's because he's sitting with his arm around Alyssa

Benson, the most popular girl in the seventh grade. Kylie joins her best friend, Jen, and they immediately start laughing and talking a mile a minute. I notice Jonathan, the kid who asked Kylie to the dance, watching her with sad eyes. I feel sorry for him. I find an empty seat halfway down the aisle and look out the window. At the next stop Ruby gets on. I can't help notice the large duffel over her arm, no doubt packed with the perfect gymnastics-tryout outfit. She doesn't even glance my way and takes a seat in the second row.

The next stop is Stephanie's. She's going to be really surprised to see me. When she gets on – also with a duffel on her shoulder – I call her name but the bus is too loud and people keep jumping up to touch the beach ball that's flying through the air. Stephanie heads directly for Ruby and sits down. They bend their heads together and start laughing about something, so I resist the urge to call out again. Instead, I slide down in my seat and pout. It's bad enough to have to take the bus on your birthday. To have to take the bus on your birthday while watching your best friend sit with someone else is almost as bad as being attacked by a balloon.

When we arrive at school I wait at the bottom of the stairs for Stephanie.

"Hey, Birthday Girl!" she says as she steps off.

Ruby, the best-friend stealer, follows, and also wishes me a happy birthday. I know she's just being nice because Stephanie is here. I was the only girl in our class who didn't get an invitation to Ruby's birthday party last year, even though I had invited her to mine. Mine and Leo's that is. Not that I even remember if she came since I left so fast.

"Didn't you see me on the bus?" I blurt out, looking only at Stephanie.

She takes a step back. "Huh? You were on the bus?"

I nod and point at Kylie, who is now stepping off. "Mom has a big meeting and my dad's not feeling well, so we had to take the bus."

Ruby mumbles something about going to the gym to practise and slinks away. Stephanie links her arm in mine. "I didn't see you, I swear. I'd have sat with you."

I relax. Of course she would have. After all, she did choose to stay friends with me over Leo, so that says a lot. We head towards the front door, arm in arm.

"Hey, where's your outfit?" she asks.

At first I think she's talking about my costume for the party. But why would I wear that to school? "What do you mean?"

"For tryouts. I told you to bring something cool."

There's that word again: cool. "First of all, you didn't tell me that. And second, I don't have anything cool."

"I didn't tell you?"

I shake my head.

"Oh. You'll just have to wear your gym clothes then."

"That's what I was planning." We round the corner towards our lockers and I see a sign posted for marching band auditions. It's the exact same time as gymnastics. I give a little sigh as we hurry past it.

I can see the streamers on my locker from halfway down the hall. I turn to Stephanie in surprise. "When did you have a chance to do that?"

"Do what?" She follows where I'm pointing, and then slowly grins. "Oh that? After school yesterday."

Her slight on the school bus is now forgiven.

No one has decorated my locker before, and secretly I always hoped someone would. I give her a hug. She hesitates for a second, then runs down the hall to her own locker with a backwards wave. I stand for a minute and admire the purple streamers, and the big HAPPY BIRTHDAY letters made out of different coloured paper. It must have taken her a long time to do this. I rest my backpack on the floor and notice that a few lockers away, a Tootsie Roll Pop is lying next to the wall. I bend down to look closer. It's a green apple one. My favourite. Was it supposed to be left in front of *my* locker like a birthday gift? I look around and don't see any of the kids whose lockers are nearby. I almost pick it up, and then think better of it. If it's not for me, and someone saw me take it, I'd be really embarrassed.

I put in my locker combination and pull on the metal handle. I pull harder. It's stuck! I try the combination again. The bell rings for first period, and I still can't get it open. Good thing I took all my books home last night, otherwise I wouldn't have them for my classes. I had planned to get ahead in my homework so I wouldn't have to do any tonight, but that plan hadn't quite worked.

Grumbling, I pick up my backpack and run to

class. History is the only class Leo and I have together, and I hate bringing any attention to myself. Ms. Gottlieb makes a big deal if you're late. Fortunately she's busy writing on the board and doesn't see me come in. Manoeuvering through the desks as quietly as possible, I slide into my seat. From across the room, I swear I can feel Leo's eyes on me. I want to turn around and wish him a happy birthday, but even now, a year later, his mean words still feel fresh. I keep my eyes glued to the board where the words POP QUIZ suddenly become clear.

Pop quiz?? My stomach sinks. I'm not good at pop quizzes, but Leo's even worse. I steal a glance at him while pretending to tuck my hair behind my ear. He looks pale.

Ms Gottlieb takes attendance, and then tells us to put everything on the floor. The class groans collectively.

"Don't worry," she says, "if you don't get higher than a seventy-five on the test, you can retake it after school. Well, not the same exact version, of course."

Stay after school on my birthday? No, thanks!

Ms. Gottlieb hands out the quiz, and it's actually not too bad. The last question is the only one that stumps me. Which of the following items CANNOT be found in the Willow Falls Historical Society Museum:

a. a bed warmer

b. a stuffed raccoon

c. a wooden crib

d. the journal of the town's founding father

The Historical Society is really just a little house decorated to look like it did a hundred years ago. I've been there a dozen times on school field trips, but old furniture is pretty boring and I've never paid much attention. I decide to take my chances and say that there's no creepy stuffed raccoon. I probably would have noticed that!

When the quiz is over, we have to switch papers with the person next to us. Ms Gottlieb reads the correct answers. Turns out there WAS a stuffed raccoon! The journal was the right answer. Oh well. I hand Jimmy Dawson his 94 and he gives me my 86 and whispers, "Happy birthday". Jimmy and I used to be good friends, but after The Fight, he's mostly been Leo's friend. I don't blame him for choosing Leo. He *is* a boy, after all. I thank him and risk another glance behind me. Leo's holding his head in his hands. Not a good sign.

By lunch time my shoulders are about to fall off my body. My bag feels ten times heavier. I've GOT to get my locker fixed. On my way to lunch I stop at the office and have to fill out a request form in order for the janitor to fix it.

I hobble to the cafeteria, bent forward like I'm hiking up a mountain with a pup tent on my back, and collapse into a chair at our usual table. Carrying six classes' worth of books has made me really hungry. I remember with a groan that my lunch is still sitting in the refrigerator at home. I dig around for loose change but all I find is forty-five cents. Stephanie shows up with Emma and Tracy Becker. Even when Leo and I WERE still friends, we never had lunch together. The boy/girl division in the cafeteria is non-negotiable. Emma and Tracy are twins and most people can't tell them apart. It's pretty easy if you know where to look. Emma has a freckle next to her right ear and Tracy doesn't. Also, Tracy only eats organic vegan food, and Emma only eats things made of sugar. The four of us sit together at lunch every day.

I share my lunch-less plight with them, but between the four of us, we can only come up with a dollar twenty. So my lunch consists of half a soggy tuna sandwich from Stephanie, a yodel from Emma, and three carrots from Tracy. It wouldn't be so bad if the conversation wasn't all about the party tonight. But not MY party. *Leo*'s party!

"I heard he's having a hypnotist!"

"No way! I heard he's having a rock band!" "A giant lizard!"

OK, that's it! At the mention of a giant lizard, I push back my chair and stand, grimacing at the loud squeak.

"Are you OK?" Tracy asks.

"I just need to, um, go to the bathroom."

"I'll come with you," Stephanie says, carefully placing her half-sandwich back in the bag.

"No, that's OK. I'll just be a minute." I leave before she can point out that we NEVER go to the bathroom alone. On the way over to the cafeteria monitor's desk I hear a table of girls talking about Leo's party. Who's going with who,

who's wearing what, what they got him as a gift. I can swear their voices cut off when they see me approach. I grit my teeth and hurry past their table.

I quickly sign for a hall pass and push open the nearest door. It feels good to be alone in the quiet hallway. Since I don't really have to use the bathroom, I decide to make one big loop around the school. As I pass the sixth grade science lab, a boy who looks kind of like a bee in a bright yellow shirt and black pants, runs out crying and crashes right into me! His glasses go flying off and careen into the lockers. He drops to the floor and starts patting the ground to find them. This kid must REALLY have bad eyesight! I bend down and hand him the glasses. He takes them and keeps sniffling.

"Um, are you all right?"

He nods repeatedly, and then starts shaking his head, instead. "I left my science project at home by mistake. Mr Collins said if anyone didn't bring it in today, our grade would drop a whole letter!"

"Can one of your parents bring it to you?"

He wipes his nose on his forearm and shakes his head again. "They both work in the city."

It's a little weird that a sixth grader is confiding in me. "What's the assignment?" I ask.

"We . . . *sniffle* . . . have to . . . *sniffle* . . . draw the periodic table. You know, with all the elements and stuff."

I really *don't* know. I shake my head. "I'm sorry, I thought maybe I could help somehow, but we haven't got to that stuff yet. We're still on the amoeba."

He wipes his nose again on his sleeve. I wish I had a tissue to give him because his sleeves are not a pretty sight. The door to the classroom opens and his teacher, Mr Collins, pokes his head out. "Have you collected yourself yet?" The boy nods, and without even a glance at me, hurries back into the room. I sure hope I don't have Mr Collins for science next year.

I hurry back to the cafeteria before the bell rings and use my dollar twenty to buy milk. I try to act normal while I scarf down the last of my meal. I decide to just smile, and not think any more about birthdays. This gets harder when my friends bring out a chocolate cupcake with a fake candle on it and all start singing "Happy Birthday".

"Make a wish, make a wish!" they chant.

I point out that the candle is made of plastic, but pretend to blow it out anyway. They clap, and it spreads to the tables around us. People I don't even know are clapping. I look up and catch Leo's eye a few tables away. He smiles at me, almost like he knew what my wish was. My stomach clenches. I quickly look away and busy myself trying to cut the cupcake into four pieces. This is not an easy task and I wind up making such a mess that the cupcake becomes an unrecognizable pile of brown crumbs and blobs of icing.

We eat it anyway.

Chapter Five

Finally, sometime between seventh and eighth periods, my locker gets fixed. I know this because I tried in vain to open it before seventh, and when I go back after eighth, it suddenly glides right open. My birthday streamers are in tatters from people pulling at them as they walked by, but that's OK. The janitor takes everything down at the end of the day.

After stuffing most of the contents of my backpack into my locker, I reluctantly head to the gym for gymnastic tryouts. As I pass the guidance counsellor's office, who do I see, but Leo again! Why is it that when you're avoiding someone, you see them that much more? Leo's face is red, and he has a tissue in his hand. His allergies must be acting up. They always do this time of year. I tighten my grip on my backpack, prepared to flee. But this time he doesn't see me, so I don't have to pretend not to see him. I stare instead at the sign for the marching band audition that starts in five minutes. I'd so much rather be banging on my drum than flipping through the air right now. As though I COULD flip through the air.

I hurry to the locker room and throw on my gym shorts and a plain white tee. I'm slipping on my white Keds when Ruby comes in. She's wearing a shiny red leotard with shiny red leggings. She looks like she could be competing at the Olympics. In my ratty gym clothes I look like I could be handing out towels in the locker room at the Olympics.

"Excited?" she asks, pausing to re-lace one of her sneakers on the bench.

"About what?" I hope she's not asking me about my party, since I didn't invite her. When she didn't invite me to hers last year, I figured OK, she just doesn't like me. And I crossed her off my future birthday list.

She rolls her eyes. "About tryouts!"

"Oh. Um, not really. I'm not that good."

I expect her to look pleased at this, but she just

shrugs. "Don't worry about it. Maybe some of the other girls will freeze under the pressure and you'll look better."

I force myself to give a little chuckle, even though her comment was kind of mean.

I follow her out to the gym. Stephanie is warming up. I hold my breath as she executes a perfect back handspring. None of the other competitors clap, but I do. I wish Tracy and Emma were trying out, too. That would make this less horrible. But they have a built-in excuse. They help out at their parents' flower shop after school. Plus Emma is worried that if she made the team Coach Lyons would make her stop eating candy. And if Emma stopped eating candy, Emma would stop *eating*.

Since she's already on the floor, Coach Lyons tells Stephanie to go first. She repeats her nearly flawless routine and this time a few more kids clap along with me. Breathless and grinning, Stephanie runs over to join me on the bleachers. Coach Lyons calls Ruby next. Ruby tightens the hair band around her perfect ponytail, and does four cartwheels in a row, just to get to the spot where her routine is supposed to start! I don't understand why Stephanie likes her. Ruby's routine goes off without a hitch. She's a little wobbly on her landings, but not too bad. I wish my only problem was a wobbly landing.

"Amanda Ellerby," Coach Lyons calls, checking my name off on her clipboard.

"Remember to keep smiling," Stephanie whispers as I slowly stand up. I plaster a smile on my face. I hope it doesn't look as fake as it feels.

The music starts and I relax. I can do the first few things pretty well. The somersaults, the handstand, the cartwheel. I can even do a back walkover. I take my time on these, drawing them out as long as possible. But it's time for the back handspring and all I can hear is my heart beating. As I stand there, arms raised by my ears in preparation, I'm momentarily blinded by the glare of Ruby's shiny red outfit glowing in the sunlight that streams through the gym windows. I close my eyes and try to focus on everything Stephanie taught me. But all I recall is something about swinging my arms, and remembering to smile. So I swing my arms. And I smile. And I swing my arms some more.

"Any time now, Amanda," Coach Lyons says, pointing to her watch.

But all I can do is swing my arms. Oh, and smile. From the bleachers I hear Stephanie yell, "Come on, Amanda. You can do it!"

But I can't. I can't do it. I'm totally frozen. Coach Lyons makes some kind of mark on her clipboard and then blows her whistle. "Jana Morling, you're up."

Jana is a small girl who just transferred here last month. She stands up, but hesitates. She looks at me, then back at the coach. I finally unfreeze enough to step off the mat so she can take her turn. I feel like I'm in one of those dreams where you're taking a big test but you realize you've missed class all year. Did I really just freeze like that and not even try? Stephanie's probably really mad. She did so great, she'll definitely make the team. And then she'll be friends with the popular girls and I won't.

I feel like I have a bowling ball stuck in my stomach.

I quickly change back into my clothes and run through the hall towards the front door. I pass the kids coming out of the band auditions with their instruments in black cases and that only makes me feel worse. I sit on the concrete steps of the school to wait for Stephanie's mom, who's driving us home. I'm leaning against the railing, wondering how I'm going to explain to her what happened, when she pulls up in their Jeep. She waves and gets out of the car.

"How'd it go, honey?"

"Not so good. But Stephanie did great."

She pats me on the shoulder. "I'm sure you did fine."

I shake my head. She digs into her pocketbook and pulls out a cherry lollipop. She holds it out to me.

"Thanks," I say, taking it. Stephanie has a four-year-old sister who likes to throw tantrums in public, so her mom always has a stash of in-case-of-emergency lollipops. I've just unwrapped it and stuck it in my mouth when Stephanie runs out of the building, followed by Ruby. I brace myself.

"What happened to you?" she asks, not even saying hi to her mom.

"I don't know. I guess I froze." Out of the corner of my eye I can see Ruby hiding a smile behind her notebook. Did she set me up? I'm about to accuse her of mentioning the whole freezing thing just to psych me out, but it doesn't really matter. It's not like I would have been able to do the stupid back handspring anyway. I wish

Stephanie would stop looking at me with that mixture of pity and disappointment.

Stephanie's mom puts her arm around me again. "Come on, Stephanie. It's Amanda's birthday today. Go easy on her."

I smile gratefully.

Stephanie sighs. "I just wanted us to be on the team together, that's all. It's not going to be the same without you."

"You made it!" I shout, genuinely happy for her.

She nods, unable to keep from grinning. "So did Ruby."

Ruby grins too, and they slap hands. I follow them out to the car and have to listen the whole way home to how excited they are. Why couldn't I be more coordinated? I wonder which parent I can blame for passing down the uncoordination gene. If there is such a thing.

When we get to my house Stephanie walks with me up to the door. "So you're OK? About me being on the team?"

I nod. "It's fine. We can't always be good at the same things."

She gives me a hug. "Hey, I'll see you in a few hours. I can't wait to show you my costume!"

Ack! My party! I had actually forgotten! And

it starts in two hours! I glance in the driveway to see if my mom's car is there, but it's not. I use my key to let myself in. I only get two steps inside when the shape on the couch moans. It's Dad, still in his robe. That's not a good sign.

"Dad? Are you OK?"

He groans. "I feel like I was hit by a truck."

I run over to the couch and kneel down. "Were you? Hit by a truck?"

He shakes his head. Sweat rolls down his cheek. "Just an expression, honey. I'm really sick though. Fever, the whole shebang. I don't think I'm going to be much help tonight at your party."

"It's OK," I assure him. "It's not that big a deal. I'm only eleven. It's not even that big a birthday."

He shakes his head again. It clearly takes an effort. "Every birthday is a big birthday. It's a celebration of your birth. It reminds me and your mother of how happy we were eleven years ago today when you entered the world."

"Really? I thought it was all about the gifts."

He narrows his eyes at me to make sure I'm joking. "I'd laugh, but I'd just start choking."

"I'll get you some water." I stand to go, but he stops me.

"Honey, I know this is a hard birthday for you,

but I hope you still have a good time."

I don't answer at first. Dad never even asked what happened at last year's party. He simply stopped mentioning Leo's name when he saw how upset I was. "Thanks, Dad. I'm sure I will."

In the two minutes it takes me to get him a glass of water, he falls back asleep.

I'm definitely going to need a new DJ for my party.

Chapter Six

This has got to be the itchiest dress I've ever had the misfortune of wearing. And the red shoes are so tight I can't feel my toes. I hobble into my parents' room.

"Is it too late to cancel the party?" I demand.

Mom's sitting at her vanity table brushing her hair. "What, honey? Yes, of course it's too late to cancel the party. Your friends will be here in fifteen minutes."

I sigh and sit on the edge of her bed. "I just wish we could have done something, I don't know, smaller. Like a slumber party or something."

She puts down her brush. "Then why didn't you say that when I asked what you wanted to do?"

I shrug. "I dunno."

But I *do* know. I didn't want to seem lame. Like

Leo would have a big party and I wouldn't, and everyone would be talking about it.

"It'll be fine," Mom says. She leans over and straightens my collar. "And you look adorable."

I shake my head sadly. "I don't."

"You do," she insists. "Ask your father."

"You look great," a rumbly voice wheezes from behind me. I jump up and whirl around. The unmoving lump in the bed that I thought was pillows is my father!

"Dad?"

"Youngest daughter? Is that you?" He reaches a shaky hand out from under the covers. "Come closer in case this is the last time I see you."

Mom laughs. "Honestly, Stuart. You're the worst sick person I've ever known."

Dad coughs and says, "You'll regret saying that when I'm gone."

Mom rolls her eyes.

"Hey, how did the presentation go?" I ask her.

Mom's smile fades instantly. "Not my best," she admits. "You better go do your hair, it's almost seven."

My hand reaches up instinctively. "I *did* do my hair."

"Oh," she says.

"Have fun tonight," Dad croaks.

I frown. "I'm not promising anything."

I run into Kylie in the hall. She's dressed as the Little Mermaid. I try to swallow the jealousy at how pretty her costume is, but it's hard.

"Happy birthday," she says.

Finally!

"Thanks," I mutter. "I hate my costume."

She looks me up and down. "Yeah, it's pretty bad."

"Gee, thanks! Way to make me feel better."

"Why did you pick it then?" she asks, adjusting her long red wig.

"I didn't pick it. Mom did."

"Look at it this way, at least you don't have to worry about anyone else dressing like Alice in Wonderland."

"I'm not Alice in Wonderland!"

She wrinkles her brows. "Who are you then?"

I hold up the wicker picnic basket. "I'm Dorothy? From *The Wizard of Oz*?"

She snaps her fingers. "That's right! I see it now. I used to love that movie."

Figures.

* * * * * * * * * * * *

The guests start arriving a few minutes after seven. The Disney princesses are well-represented. The boys seem to be either Freddy Krueger from the *Nightmare on Elm Street* movies or baseball players from *Field of Dreams*. Two girls are wearing the Fiona costume I had wanted and I eye them with jealousy. Tracy and Emma are Oompa-Loompas. They look amazing in white overalls, brown T-shirts and orange faces. Plus, I think most of Emma's outfit is edible. She pulls a Hershey's Kiss off her belt and presses it into my hand. Two girls from fifth period English are dressed as characters from the movie version of *Hamlet* that we watched in class last month. Stephanie is an elf with pointy ears and a long silvery cape.

"What movie are you from?" I ask, taking the gift bag from her hands.

"*Lord of the Rings*. I'm Arwen."

"You look great," I tell her, even though I've never seen the movie. Mom said it's too violent for me. I would argue, but after being terrified by a SpongeBob balloon, I'm pretty sure she's right.

Dad insisted on dragging himself out of bed and manning the CD player, which really could just man itself. He's wearing the cowboy costume

Mom rented for him. Every few minutes, he has a sneezing fit and his hat flies off and everyone in the room stops talking. It's highly embarrassing. Mom is wearing a Cruella de Vil outfit. She looks good in black. She keeps answering her cell phone though, and it's getting annoying. I understand she has a really important job, but what could be so important on a Friday night? During your daughter's birthday party?

Dad spent a lot of time burning CDs of movie theme songs, but they're not really danceable. Everyone's mostly standing around eating chips and M&Ms. After what feels like an eternity of making small talk, I glance up at the clock. It's almost 8:00, and half the people aren't here. Only three of the boys I invited have shown up. Dad was supposed to organize the games, but he's sitting down on the couch, a glazed expression on his pale face. Kylie disappeared long ago.

I pull Stephanie aside and whisper, "Where is everyone?"

She looks around the room uneasily. "I'm not sure."

I have the feeling she knows more than she's saying. I squeeze her arm. Hard.

"OK, OK. I think they went to Leo's party instead." I release my grip. "Oh."

"On top of everything else, he supposedly has some big football player there. You know, giving tips on throwing and stuff."

My head swims with this new information.

"Um, Amanda?"

I don't answer.

"Um, would you mind a ton if I went, too? Just for a little while? I'll come back, I promise."

At first I think she's kidding. "But you don't even like football."

She looks down at the carpet. "It's just that Mena and Heather and Jess and the rest of the girls who made the gymnastics team are there, and if I don't go it wouldn't look good. I want them to know I'm a team player. You know how it is."

"I guess so," I say, hoping my voice doesn't crack. I just want to go upstairs and cry. I tug hard at my collar, which is so scratchy it has made my neck red and blotchy. I want to ask since when is Leo friends with those girls, but I don't really want to know.

Stephanie gives me a quick hug and slips out just before Mom brings out my cake. I make the same wish I made at lunch over the cupcake. I wish I had never walked by Leo's room that night. I wish so hard I almost fool myself into believing that when I open my eyes, all this will be gone and Leo and I will be in the middle of one of our great parties, where no one has to pretend to be having fun.

Nope.

The party drags on until finally the parents start arriving. I pray that Mom doesn't invite them in for cake, and thankfully she doesn't. The basement quickly empties. Struggling to choke back tears, I toss the used plastic cups into the garbage, one by one. Even the table piled with presents can't cheer me up. Although there really are a lot of presents considering only eight kids showed up. I lift up the cards. One after another are names of kids I invited but who didn't show up. At least I thought they hadn't shown up. That's weird.

Mom's voice wafts down the stairs towards me. She's on the phone, as usual. "No, I haven't told Amanda yet. I didn't want to ruin her party." She reaches the bottom of the stairs and catches sight of me standing by the gifts. She backs up half a step, looking surprised. "I'll call you back later," she says, closing her cell.

"What was that about?" I ask, sinking into the couch.

She sits down next to me and takes a deep breath. "I was fired tonight."

It takes a few seconds for her words to sink in. I sit up straight. "Fired? You? Can they do that?"

"They can and they did."

"But why?"

She sighs. "It's complicated. I lost a very important account this morning. I knew a lot was riding on this one."

"They didn't like your ideas? But you always have good ideas." I pull at my collar again. "Except maybe for this costume!"

The sides of her mouth curl up, but she quickly frowns again. "They didn't even get to see my ideas. I spent weeks working on the mock-up for the campaign, but I left it at home. There wasn't time to redo it."

"But I saw you leave this morning, and you had the poster rolled up under your arm."

She shakes her head sadly. "No, what I had was your sister's science project. If the client had wanted to learn how a solid turns into a gas, I'd have been all set." She starts to laugh, but it's not a happy laugh. "Enough about me. I'll find another job, not to worry," she says with finality. "So, did you enjoy your party? "

I open my mouth to answer, but don't know what to say. She already feels bad enough, I don't want to add to it. So I just nod. I don't know if she believes me, but she doesn't press it.

"You sure got a lot of gifts," she says, gesturing to the table. "They kept showing up all night."

My eyes widen. "People just dropped them off at the door? And didn't even come in?"

She hesitates, then presses her lips together, which is what she does when she doesn't want to answer. I can't believe this. "I'm going to go to bed now, OK?"

"Don't you want to open them?"

I shake my head. "I'll do it tomorrow." I hurry upstairs before she says anything else. The light is already off in Kylie's room, which is surprising since she's usually up IM-ing her friends at this time of night. I lock my door and kick off the shoes, which have given me blisters on both heels. I wrestle the dress to the ground, and kick it under my desk.

I guess Stephanie's not coming back tonight. I don't really want to talk to anyone anyway. I hope she had fun with her new gymnastics friends. No one in my family even asked me how tryouts went. I put on my most comfortable pyjamas and climb into bed. Is this what every birthday from now on is going to be like? Even though I'm still mad at Leo, I hope he had a better time at his party than I had at mine.

I switch off my lamp and close my eyes. At least tomorrow's Saturday and I won't have to deal with seeing everyone at school who blew off my party. I lie still, waiting for sleep to come. But something's not right. I switch the lamp back on, hop out of bed, and shut SpongeBob in the closet.

Ah, that's better.

Chapter Seven

My first thought when I turn off my alarm is how happy I am that my birthday is over and done with. My second thought is *Why is my alarm going off on a Saturday?* I must have set it out of habit. I close my eyes again and snuggle under the covers. It's almost worth waking up this early on the weekend, just to know I can go back to sleep.

I'm about to drift off again when the sound of Kylie's door opening and closing startles me. Why is she up so early? Maybe she forgot to turn off her alarm, too. I glance at the clock. It's still before seven. Out of the corner of my eye, I spy something moving in the middle of my room. I bolt upright. It's the SpongeBob balloon, waving happily at me. I rub my eyes and then whirl around to check the closet door. Still shut. Is this why Kylie's up so early? She woke up to play a trick on me? We don't really have a trick-playing kind of relationship. I'm not sure what kind of relationship we have. We used to get along pretty well, until a few years ago. Now all she cares about is talking to her friends. Sometimes I think she forgets she even *has* a younger sister.

Now that I'm awake, I have to go to the bathroom. On the way, I put SpongeBob back in the closet and place some heavy sneakers on top of his cardboard feet. He's not going anywhere now. Kylie's door is open, like it was yesterday. I stick my head in to ask her about the balloon, but she's not there. Her diary's out on the floor again. She's either getting more trusting or more forgetful.

I'm on my way back from the bathroom when Mom steps out of her room, fully dressed in her business suit. "Amanda, why aren't you dressed? The bus leaves in ten minutes!"

All I can think to say to this odd statement is, "The bus?"

She nods, fastening her necklace. "I'm sorry I can't take you to school. I have a big meeting. And your dad's feeling pretty sick. Now hurry up or you'll miss it."

She closes her door and I stand there, unsure

how to react. I know Mom losing her job must have been a big shock, but she's in some kind of weird denial or something. Maybe it's like the time I got six inches cut off my hair, and for days after I kept thinking it was still there.

She opens the door again. "Oh, and happy birthday, honey!" She gives me a squeeze, then says, "Now go on, get dressed."

Kylie runs upstairs in her jogging outfit as Mom closes her door again. She glances at me, taking in my pyjamas and fuzzy socks. "You better get dressed. We have to take the bus today."

Ah, OK. Now it makes sense!

"I get it!" I announce happily. "This is some kind of game. You're all trying to trick me into thinking it's a school day. Well, it's not going to work."

Kylie shrugs and goes into her room. "Whatever you say."

I smile as I climb back into bed. It's nice that they went to all this effort for me.

Five minutes later Mom bursts into the room. "Amanda! What are you doing?"

I lean up on my elbows. "It's OK, Mom. I figured it out. You can go back to bed now."

Instead, she walks over and pulls the covers

off my bed. "You have five minutes. I know you're not looking forward to your party tonight, but you've simply got to make the best of it. Now get up."

"What do you mean I'm not looking forward to my party? My party was *yesterday*!"

She flicks her wrist over to check her watch. "Amanda, I don't know what's got into you today, but I have to go. Please don't miss the bus, your dad really isn't in any condition to drive you." With that she rushes out of the room.

Wow. They're really committing to this joke! Maybe it leads to some big present for me. Like, if I get up and get dressed, then we'll all wind up going somewhere really cool for the day. Fine. I'll play along. I open my drawers and am momentarily surprised to see my clothes from yesterday clean and folded. Mom must have done it last night after I went to sleep. I get dressed quickly and run downstairs, expecting to see everyone waiting for me. But Dad's alone in the kitchen, drinking his tea in the same pyjamas as yesterday.

"Happy birthday, sweetie," he says groggily, then pauses to sneeze. "Kylie already left. You better hurry."

I wink. "Right. I better hurry. Wouldn't want

to miss the school bus!" I start out the door, but he grabs my arm.

"Don't forget this." He hands me my backpack. It's really heavy, like it was yesterday. That's weird. I put most of my books away when my locker got fixed. My parents must have weighed it down with stuff as part of their plan. I wink again as I sling it over my shoulder.

"Do you have something in your eye, honey?" Dad asks, peering at me closely. "You keep blinking strangely."

"Very funny, Dad. See you later! Or sooner!"

He stands at the door as I leave, an odd expression on his face. He's probably trying not to give away the surprise. Kylie is waiting on the corner when I get there, also wearing the same outfit she wore yesterday. I wonder how my parents bribed her into going along with all of this.

"I see you made it," she says.

I rock on my heels. "Yup."

I point at the poster under her arm. "Your science project, right? Or *is* it?"

"Or is it what?"

"Or is it Mom's presentation for her meeting?"

Kylie stares at me. "What are you talking

about?"

"How long do you think they'll make us wait?" I ask her. "You know, before they come get us?"

"The bus is only two minutes late," she says, looking down the block. "Chill out."

I smile. Kylie always was a good actress. She had the lead in the school play last year. Even though I wish I were still cosy in my bed, I'm actually enjoying myself. If my family is doing all of this to make me feel better about last night's party disaster, it's working.

"Here it comes," Kylie says, picking her bag up from the sidewalk.

I turn to look, expecting to see Mom's car. But it's the school bus! I know it's ours because it says Willow Falls Middle School on it. I'm speechless. Did they hire the bus driver to work on a Saturday? All for me? The door whooshes open, and I follow Kylie up the stairs. My stomach drops to my feet when the sounds of all the kids reach me. A beach ball narrowly misses my head. I try to pick up my feet to walk, but stumble. Everything is just like it was yesterday! Kylie's science partner, Dustin, is sitting with his arm around that girl Alyssa. Kylie ignores him and laughs with her best friend, Jen, just like yesterday. Jonathan looks on with those sad eyes. Feeling shaky and a little bit faint, I collapse in the same seat I had chosen yesterday. My head is swimming.

If this isn't a game planned by my loving family, what is this, then? Did I just dream everything that happened yesterday? My dreams are usually about me wearing pyjamas to school or forgetting to study for a test. I've never dreamed a whole DAY before, and it sure didn't feel like a dream. But how else can I explain the fact that I know everything that's about to happen? I must be psychic! Maybe I always WAS, and it's just coming out now that I'm eleven. I must be having premonitions, which was a vocabulary word in English class a few months ago. It means I'm able to predict the future. That's why all this feels so familiar. Like a serious case of déjà vu.

The bus pulls up to Ruby's stop. She climbs on with her big duffel bag and flips her hair, just like I knew she would. I wonder what other kinds of magical powers I have.

Stephanie climbs on the bus and I try out my powers on her. I send her a telepathic message telling her I'm on the bus and to come sit with me. She doesn't even glance my way. OK, so I probably don't have telepathy. Maybe I can move things with my mind. I focus on that annoying beach ball that keeps bopping from person to person. I try to get it to come to me.

It doesn't.

OK, cross that one off the list. Maybe mind reading? I turn around in my seat. Behind me is Brian Grady, a kid in my math class. "Hey, Brian," I say, "think of a number between one and ten."

He takes out his earphones. "Huh?"

I repeat my request.

"OK."

I concentrate for a second, then a number eight pops into my head. "Eight!" I announce confidently.

He shakes his head and puts his earphones back in. "Three."

I turn back around, defeated. OK, so I can't read minds. The bus is pulling up to the school now and I force myself to climb out.

"Hey, Birthday Girl!" Stephanie says when I reach the bottom of the stairs.

Ruby mumbles happy birthday, too, but I ignore her. I'm feeling really uneasy and even a little nauseous. I'm tempted to tell Stephanie what's going on, but I don't understand it myself, and Ruby would just laugh at me. Having psychic powers can be a lonely existence. "Didn't you see me on the bus?" I finally ask.

She takes a step back. "Huh? You were on the bus?"

I nod and watch Kylie step off, wearing the same blank expression she wore yesterday. I turn back to Stephanie. "My mother has a big meeting, and my dad's not feeling well."

Just like I knew she would, she assures me she would have sat with me. A few minutes later I have to pretend to be surprised at my decorated locker, and then even though I knew it was coming, I actually AM surprised when I can't pull the locker door open. I seem to know everything that's going to happen, even down to little tiny details. I glance to my left. Yup, even the lollipop is there. My unease is starting to turn to fear. I'm not sure I WANT to be psychic any more.

The bell rings while I'm still standing in front of my jammed locker. I'm now late for class, like I knew I would be. I slide into my seat. The teacher steps aside, revealing the announcement of the pop quiz. Even though I know the answers, when the quiz hits my desk I decide to mark down the same choices I made before. I'm scared of what might happen if I change things.

I get my same 86. I risk another glance at Leo. His head is in his hands, like yesterday. If there's anyone I'd want to tell about my new powers, it would be him. Well, it *would* have been him. Before he betrayed me. I'm sure Stephanie wouldn't laugh at me, but she probably wouldn't believe me, either.

The rest of the morning goes by in a haze. On my way to lunch I stop to report my locker problem and realize that I forgot my lunch. Ugh! What's the point of predicting something in advance if it's not going to save me some trouble? My friends have the same amount of extra change, the conversation about Leo's party is the same, and I have the same need to leave the cafeteria. The déjà vu continues as the crying boy knocks into me again and we have the same conversation. Periodic table, snot on his shirtsleeve, amoebas, mean science teacher. Then cupcake, singing, wishing, and that smile from Leo. I wish I could just hide under the lunch table until all this goes away.

School finally ends. I dump most of my books

into my locker and tuck in the remaining streamers. I desperately want to go home, but I'm stuck going to gymnastics tryouts. Leo, nose red from sneezing, is about to push open the door of the guidance counsellor's office. I hurry past even though I know he won't see me. I don't want to take any chances.

Twenty minutes later I'm standing in the middle of the gym, swinging my arms over and over again. The familiar bright light glinting off Ruby's red outfit is blinding me. Yup, this moment is just as horrible as it was before. Standing there under the eyes of the coach, of Stephanie and Ruby and the rest of the kids trying out, of the kids who're already ON the team, I know this feeling of humiliation isn't something I could have dreamed up, psychic or not. I start to shake again and lower my arms for good.

On the ride home when Stephanie says she made the team I pretend I hadn't known and congratulate her. When Dad says he feels like he got hit by a truck I pretend I don't know what he means. And when I'm faced with the itchy Dorothy costume I grit my teeth and slip it over my head. But when I put on the horrid red shoes, something feels different from before. Up till now everything's unfolded exactly like I knew it would. I knew that the shoes would be tight when I put them on, but they're more than tight. They really, really hurt. I pull them off again and examine my feet. Both ankles have blisters on them in the exact spots where the shoes rub against the back of my heels. I hadn't felt them earlier in my socks and sneakers. I touch the blisters. Ouch! My head starts swimming again. Doesn't this prove that I didn't just IMAGINE wearing the shoes before? Doesn't this prove that I really *did* wear them? I break out in a sweat. The sweat doesn't help with the itchiness of the costume.

I can't deal with this now. I have a party to get through. Again.

With shaking hands, I pull out two Band-Aids from the medicine cabinet and put them on my heels. I slip on the shoes, which feel a little more bearable now. Kylie walks out of her room in her Little Mermaid costume, and I realize I've taken so much time getting ready that I never made it into Mom and Dad's room to complain about the party.

"Are you OK?" Kylie asks, peering closely at

me. "You've been weird all day. I mean, weirder than usual."

I back up a few steps. "It's been a weird day. I don't feel very well."

She reaches up to adjust her red mermaid wig. "Well, I'm sure you'll have fun at your party. You're only eleven once, ya know."

"I'm not so sure about that," I mutter.

The doorbell rings but I let Mom answer it. While my friends file down to the basement I lock myself in the bathroom and splash water on my face. In the movies that's what people always do when they find themselves in a situation they can't figure out. All it does for me is make the front of my costume wet.

On my way past the front door I see a shadow outside scurrying away. I open the door to find a stack of wrapped boxes and gift bags. I drag them inside and shut the door louder than probably necessary.

This time I see Kylie slip out after Mom brings down the punch and ice cream. When Stephanie asks me if it's OK to go to Leo's I barely hear her. It's like my brain is buzzing and blocking everything out.

Just when I think I'm going to lose it

completely, the party ends. I linger downstairs, waiting for Mom to come back down. I think I better tell her what's going on. But when she sees me and starts telling me about losing her job, I chicken out. I tell myself this is some bizarre once-in-a-lifetime thing, and tomorrow everything will be normal again.

Back in my room, I pull off my costume, ball it up, and throw it in the trash. I toss the shoes on top, along with the little wicker basket. I lock my door this time and double-check that the alarm clock is turned off. Then I put on my pj's, climb into bed and sink down on to the pillow. With one last glance at the closet to make sure it's securely closed, I shut my eyes tight.

I have a strange feeling the SpongeBob balloon is laughing at me.

Chapter Eight

Hurrah! I'm awake and my alarm didn't go off! I woke up all on my own, which means it must be Saturday! Whatever happened yesterday is over and done with and I can put it behind me. It must still be early because it's still dark in my room, but I'm too happy to go back to sleep. Might as well open those presents! I swing my legs off the side of the bed and bump directly into SpongeBob.

NOOOOOOO!!!!!!!!!

I grab him, stick him back in the closet, and slam the door. I hold my breath and peer into the trash can next to my desk where I threw my costume last night.

Empty.

Maybe I dreamed the last *two* days and *today* is really my birthday? Trembling, I reach down to feel the backs of my ankles. Band-Aids on both. I sit down on my bed and begin to cry. This is no dream or déjà vu. I never had psychic powers. I can finally accept that now.

Ten seconds later, my alarm beeps. I want to throw it across the room. I can't do this over again. I just can't. I crawl back into bed and throw the covers over my head. Why is every day my eleventh birthday? And why doesn't anyone else realize it? Why is this happening to *me*, of all people? I'm not special in any way. Well, I can touch my nose with my tongue, but that's pretty much it.

A little while later Mom comes in and asks me why I'm not up. I say the first thing that comes to my mind. "I don't feel well. My head hurts." It's not even a lie. My head does hurt from thinking so hard.

She feels my cheeks, cold from crying. "You do feel clammy."

"Maybe I have what Dad has," I say weakly.

"How do you know your father's sick? He was fine last night."

"I heard him coughing in his sleep," I say quickly. Then I cough a few times for good measure. "I think I'd better stay home."

She shakes her head. "Don't you have

gymnastics tryouts? And your party! You can't miss your own party!"

"I feel really sick, Mom. I don't mind not having the party. And let's face it, I'm not going to make the gymnastics team."

I can see her weighing the options. I focus on looking sickly.

"I won't be here to take care of you," she finally says. "And your father is useless when he's sick. Mrs Grayson down the street will have to take you to the doctor."

Ugh, going to the doctor is worse than school. But today I'll take it. "That's OK. I like Mrs Grayson."

Mom sighs and checks her watch. "OK, I'll call the school and the doctor, and then I have to run." She leans down and kisses me on top of my head. "Try to have a happy birthday, sweetheart. I'll call your friends' parents from my office and let them know. We'll figure out a date to reschedule your party when I get home." She closes the door behind her and I push myself up. No school today! No more pretending I don't know that a stuffed raccoon lives at the Historical Society. No more humiliating gymnastics tryouts. No more telling myself it doesn't hurt every time

I see Leo on what used to be our special day.

What a relief.

But reality returns all too fast. What am I going to do? Why is it always my birthday and never the day AFTER my birthday? I think it's time I told someone. I put on my robe and slippers and go off in search of Dad. I find him on a stool at the kitchen counter, reading his paper.

"Happy birthday, honey!" he says, reaching into his robe pocket for a tissue.

"Uh-huh. Can I talk to you?"

"Of course." He blows his nose. "How are you feeling? You must be pretty sick to want to cancel your party."

I shrug, unable to lie to him. "How 'bout you?"

He points to his nose. It's red and raw already.

"That's pretty gross, Dad."

He takes a long sip of tea, studying me over the rim. I squirm a bit. "So let me guess what you want to talk about," he says, laying the cup down. "You want to admit you cancelled your party tonight so you don't have to compete with Leo's. Mom told me he's having a pretty big bash."

It would be so much easier to tell him he's right. I shake my head.

"Really? OK. What's up then?"

"Um, you know how it's my eleventh birthday today?"

He nods. "I do."

Here comes the hard part. I take a deep breath. "The thing is . . . yesterday was my birthday, too. And the day before."

"Sorry, come again?"

"My birthday is, like, repeating itself. Every time I wake up, it's Friday, June fifth again." It doesn't sound any less strange saying it the second time.

Dad folds his paper neatly, tucks it under his arm, and stands up. "Honey," he says kindly, putting his arm around my shoulders. "I know this fight with Leo has been hard on you. He's been like a brother to you, and now, well, he's not in your life."

Huh? Didn't he hear me? "Dad, I already told you, this isn't about Leo."

He gives my shoulders a squeeze. "You probably have a pretty good fever, too. I was delirious around three o'clock this morning." He steers me out of the kitchen towards the stairs. "You just need a good nap. I'll wake you when it's time to get dressed for the doctor."

"But—"

"Get some rest." He leaves me with a final pat on the head.

My shoulders sag as I walk back to my room. I hadn't expected him not to believe me. I guess it's just too crazy to be true. But how come it is, then?

I try for over an hour to get back to sleep, but my head is spinning. Unfamiliar with rule breaking, I still feel guilty for making my parents think I'm sick. But actually, if this is the third time I've relived Friday, then today really should be *Sunday*. And what do people do on Sundays? They relax. I deserve to relax, too.

The Dorothy costume is lying on my desk where it always is in the morning. This time I pick it up and smile. "I won't be seeing YOU today!" I declare, scrunching it into my drawer. I push aside the jeans and T-shirt I'd worn over the last two days. If I'm not going to follow my usual routine, I might as well wear something different, too. Even though my life has gone from boring and predictable to totally insane and unreal, there's something freeing about being home on a school day. I turn on the radio and do a little dance around my room. I'd love to go downstairs to play my drums, but that doesn't seem like something a sick person could get away with.

I sit down on the bed, not sure what to do now. That's the thing about pretending to be sick. You're limited to sick-person activities, which is basically lying around watching television or reading. I could do my homework, but it would just be undone again tomorrow. I mean, when tomorrow is today again. I let out a huge sigh. What do you call it when every tomorrow is both tomorrow and today? And every *today* is both today and yesterday? I shake my head. It's enough to make me truly feel sick. I look at the clock. I've missed the pop quiz.

Well, if all I can do is watch television, I might as well get started. The one in the den downstairs is the best. As I pass Kylie's closed door I slow to a stop. Carefully, with a glance behind me to make sure Dad's not nearby, I push open the door. Yup, there it is, sitting on the floor by her bed. I pause for a second and then run in and grab the small purple notebook. KEEP OUT OR SUFFER THE CONSEQUENCES. Hey, what could Kylie do to me that would be worse than reliving this day over and over?

I skip to the end to read the latest entry. Her

handwriting is as messy as her room. Dear Diary, it starts.

Tomorrow is Amanda's 11th birthday. For some reason it's a dorky costume party, like it's Halloween in June! I'm going as the Little Mermaid. I tried on my costume last night after everyone went to bed. When I looked in the mirror it didn't even look like me, especially with the red wig on. It was kind of cool to see someone else instead of my boring face with my eyes too close together and that one ear that sticks out too far. Amanda doesn't know how lucky she is, only being eleven. I wish I were eleven again. Then I wouldn't have to worry about why Dustin likes Alyssa and not me. When he came over after dinner to work on our project, I wore my new lipstick and my new shirt from Abercrombie (which is really soft and Mom says brings out my eyes), but I don't think it worked. If he sits with Alyssa on the bus again I'll just die. Even though all my friends say not to, I'm going to ask him to the dance today during gym class. Wish me luck, diary!

I lay the book in my lap. The pages flutter closed. Just when I thought life was as weird as it's going to get, my sister surprises me by actually being insecure. Even though I haven't really thought much about the whole "wanting boys to like me" thing, it's obvious Kylie's thought about it a lot. It doesn't sound like fun. I even feel sorry for her, which is something I don't ever remember feeling before. She's wrong about it being fun to turn eleven, though. She should try doing it THREE TIMES IN A ROW! I rest the book down exactly where I found it and tiptoe back out.

I'm halfway down the stairs when the phone rings. Dad picks it up then calls my name. I hurry into the den, where he's now lying on the couch. So much for my plans of watching TV in there. "It's Stephanie," he says, handing me the phone.

I take the phone outside into the backyard and lie down on a plastic lounge chair. I've barely said hello when she starts in. "Where are you? Don't you know it's your birthday? Everyone's asking for you. Your locker's decorated, Emma brought you a cupcake for lunch time, and most important," she raises her voice, "WE HAVE TRYOUTS TODAY!"

I wait till she's run out of steam. Then I cough. "I'm sick. Party's off. No tryouts. I'm sorry."

"What? How can you be sick? I just saw you last night. You were fine."

A yellow bird flies by. It's a really nice day out. I hadn't appreciated that before, when I was stuck in school. I cough again. "I woke up with it, there's nothing I can do about it. And something tells me I wouldn't have done very well in tryouts."

She doesn't say anything for a minute. "Are you doing this because of Leo?"

"No!" I yell a bit too loudly. "It has nothing to do with him. Why does everyone keep asking me that? "

"Is it because you really wanted to try out for marching band?"

I sigh. "No, seriously, I'm just really not feeling well today. But good luck at the tryouts, I know you'll do great."

"It won't be the same without you," she insists.

"Where are you calling me from, by the way?" Neither of us is allowed a cell phone until we're twelve.

"I snuck into the guidance counsellor's office to use her phone," she says, suddenly lowering her voice. "She's coming down the hall, I better go. Hey, wait." She pauses for a second. "Mrs Philips left her appointment book open. It says here Leo has an appointment today after school."

"Yeah, I saw him come out of there yesterday. Probably meeting about next year's schedule."

"He was here yesterday, too?" I hear pages flipping. "It doesn't say that in the book."

Oops! "Oh, right, I'm just confused. You better go. You don't want to get caught."

"OK," she whispers. "Feel better and I'll call you after tryouts." She hangs up right as I hear, "Young lady, what are you doing in my office? "

I click off the phone and lay it down next to me. I hope Stephanie doesn't get into trouble. Leaning back in the chair, I tilt my face to the sun until I feel its warmth spread across my cheeks. I could get used to this.

After a few more minutes of relishing the fact that I'm not in maths class right now, I go back inside and scarf down two muffins and a tall glass of orange juice. Dad is snoring on the couch. Realizing I left the phone by the lounge chair, I go out to retrieve it. The gymnastics mat that Stephanie loaned me is still spread out on the lawn. Now that I don't have to deal with the pressure of doing a back handspring in front of the coach, it could be fun to see if I can do it on my own. Dad's sleeping, so he won't see me doing something sick people shouldn't do. I pull off my socks and grip the edges of the mat with my toes. OK, bend knees, power down with arms, and go!

I land flat on my back. I may have just attempted my last back handspring.

"Ahem," a woman's voice says.

Chapter Nine

I shield the sun from my eyes and look up. First I see the work boots, then the jeans, then the red flannel shirt, then the silver-and-black hair. Mrs Grayson. She's always dressed for gardening, even on a warm day like this. Since her husband died a few years ago, she pretty much gardens all day. "Um, hi," I say, reddening.

"I'm glad to see you're feeling better," she says, as I hurriedly put my socks back on. "Your mother had you at death's door."

I redden some more and look down. "Yes, I'm feeling a little better."

"Well, we'd better keep your appointment anyway, just to make sure."

I nod, still not meeting her gaze. "Let me get my shoes."

A few minutes later I'm standing in her driveway waiting for her to back her car out of the garage. I expected her to drive something sensible and environmentally friendly. Instead she backs out in a bright orange Jaguar. My mouth falls open.

I cautiously get in the car, afraid to touch the wood or leather, which is what everything seems to be made of. It feels like I'm sitting on a cloud. She laughs when she sees my expression.

"I call this little beauty 'Late-life Crisis'. A car like this has got to have a name, you know. I never had a midlife crisis because I was too happy, so that's where she gets her name. It was either this car or a tattoo."

"A tattoo? Wow!" Boy, you never really know people.

She laughs again. "I was just kidding on the tattoo."

I redden again. "Oh. Right. Well, it's a really nice car."

She pats the dashboard fondly. "Thank you."

We don't talk much on the five-minute drive. I cough once or twice, but my heart isn't in it. Dr Frieling sees me right away, and I try not to gag on the flat stick he lays on my tongue. He feels the sides of my neck and checks my eyes and ears.

I have to breathe deeply while he listens to my lungs. Basically the usual check-up. When he's done he announces with a grin, "Well, my dear. I believe you've had a miraculous recovery. Or what we call in this business, 'a gullible mother'."

He herds me out of the office, leaving me no chance to explain that, truly, my head *did* hurt this morning and I'm going through a very tough time. "To be on the safe side," he says as he makes a note on my chart, "lay low this weekend, don't overexert yourself. You'll no doubt be anxious to go to school on Monday." He winks, and then calls, "Next!"

Sure, easy enough for him to say. How can I lay low on a weekend THAT NEVER COMES?

"Do you want to talk about it?" Mrs Grayson asks on the ride home.

I shake my head. "You wouldn't believe me if I told you."

"Try me."

I shake my head again.

"You know, my grandmother Bessy used to be friends with your great-great-grandmother, the one you were named after."

This catches my attention. I don't know much about my dad's family. All I know is that many generations of Ellerbys grew up in Willow Falls, but my dad's parents moved away right after my dad was born. The only reason he and my mom moved back here is because Dad was offered a job nearby. Over the years I've heard a few people in town ask him if he was related to the Ellerbys who used to live in the Apple Grove section of town, and my dad will say yes, and the people will nod, sort of *knowingly*, sort of *impressed*, but I never paid much attention. And that was as far as the conversations went.

"Did your grandmother ever say anything about her?" I ask Mrs Grayson. "About my great-great-grandmother?"

"A little. She called her 'a feisty ol' broad'. She'd have to be, to keep up with her husband."

"How come? What was he like?"

Mrs Grayson turns on to our block and starts slowing down. "I don't know much about Rex. He sure turned this town on end with the whole feud." She shakes her head. "Every small town's gotta have *something* to gossip about, I guess."

Now THIS was interesting enough to make me stop thinking about my situation for a minute. "What feud? My dad never mentioned it to me."

She pulls into my driveway and shakes her

head. "I don't know anything about it. He probably doesn't, either, since his parents whisked him away from here so young. Now, you're gonna be OK? You feeling better?"

I nod. "Thanks for taking me, I really appreciate it."

"No problem," she says. "I welcome any opportunity to drive good old 'Late-life Crisis'."

I watch her swing out of my driveway and head down the block. I bet she's lonely in that house all by herself, gardening all day. I don't think she has any children. At least I never see anyone around.

Dad's still asleep on the couch when I come in. I don't worry about making noise, because it takes a lot to wake him. I make myself a turkey sandwich and settle down in his easy chair to watch daytime TV. I used to think the bizarre things that happened on soap operas could never happen in real life. But I'm living proof otherwise.

Kylie comes home from school hours later and finds me slouched in the chair, eyes glazed, finishing up a huge bag of potato chips. "You don't look very sick to me," she says.

"I feel a lot better."

She drops her backpack on to the coffee table

and casually says, "Leo stopped me in the hall today."

I sit up. "He did? Why?"

"He wanted to know why you weren't in history class. He said you missed a pop quiz."

I click off the television. "Did he say anything else?"

"What, do I have all day to chat with your ex-friends in the hall? I have my own life, you know." She turns on her heel and stomps upstairs. I'm guessing her plan to ask Dustin to the dance during gym class didn't go too well.

The phone rings and I run into the kitchen to get it. "I made it!" Stephanie's voice on the other end shouts. "I made the team! So did Ruby!"

"That's great!" I tell her with as much enthusiasm as I can muster.

"Hey, you're definitely not having your party, right?" she asks.

"Right. But you can still come over. We could watch movies." Maybe I'll get to have the birthday party I wanted after all. "We could make Rice Krispies Treats and I can play the drums and you can—"

She cuts me off. "Um, would you mind if I went to Leo's party instead? A lot of the kids on the team will be there, and it wouldn't look good if I didn't go."

"Right," I say. "Team spirit and all."

"Exactly!"

"No, I don't mind." It's not like I really have a choice.

"Thanks, you're the best. Have a great birthday. We'll celebrate on Monday, I promise."

She hangs up, and I replace the phone in the cradle. I'd settle for there BEING a Monday. I want to go down and bang on the drums until my arms hurt, but Dad is still sleeping. He might be able to sleep through the trials and tribulations of soap operas, Oprah and Judge Judy, but I think the drums would be asking a bit much. I'm trying to decide what to do with myself when Mom comes home. Her usually perfect hair has slipped out of its knot, and her papers are spilling out of her briefcase. She's holding two pizzas out in front of her. I help her bring them to the counter.

"How'd it go?" I ask, already knowing her answer.

"It wasn't my finest day," she replies, pulling some plates down from the cabinets. "But let's not talk about work. What did the doctor say?"

"He said I should take it easy this weekend." I

don't think Mom really needs to know *everything* he said.

She eyes me suspiciously, but only says, "Good thing I brought home pizza for your birthday dinner. We can eat pizza and watch whatever movie you'd like."

"That sounds great," I say, relieved.

"Unless of course you'd rather I call everyone back and tell them you're well enough for the party?"

"No! I mean, I'm fine with the pizza."

"You're sure?"

I nod. "Very sure."

Mom goes into the den to wake up Dad and sends me up to get Kylie. I knock tentatively on her door. "Time for dinner. Mom brought home pizza."

"I'm not hungry," she calls out. "Eat without me."

I wait a few seconds for her to change her mind. "C'mon, Kylie. It's my birthday." I hear scuffling in her room, then her door opens.

"Fine," she says, brushing past me.

I decide not to tell her she's wearing her Little Mermaid wig. She'll find out soon enough.

Pizza and a movie (Escape to Witch Mountain, my all-time Disney favourite) turns out to be a much better birthday than the costume party. No one rings the doorbell to drop off presents and run away, and without wearing the tight red shoes for twenty-four hours, my ankles are healing back up. The only thing that ruins it is that I keep wondering how Leo's party is going. I'm probably the one person in our grade not there.

After the movie Mom gets out the cake she had ordered for the party, and everyone sings "Happy Birthday". Once again, I wish for tomorrow to be Saturday. It's not a big wish, not extravagant. Nothing that wouldn't happen, anyway, in the natural order of things.

As soon as I blow out the candle Mom's cell phone rings. I cringe at the noise, knowing that the call holds bad news. She answers it and quickly takes it into the other room. Dad follows, looking worried.

"Aren't you going to open your presents?" Kylie asks. She's still wearing the wig. Dad had laughed when she came downstairs in it, so she pretended she intended to wear it.

I look down at the two gifts waiting for me on the kitchen table. No big pile of gifts this time. For the first time, I actually get to OPEN my eleventh birthday gifts. I linger over the wrapping, trying to stall until our parents come back. But they've now stepped outside, their voices low. I think it's going to be a while.

I open Kylie's first. It's a diary, identical to hers, but without the warning on the cover. I can't meet her eyes for a few seconds, sure that she'll be able to tell that I snooped and read hers.

"I started mine when I was eleven," she explains. "So I thought, you know, maybe you'd want one."

"Thanks." I lean in awkwardly to give her a hug, and my hand gets caught in her wig and it comes off. We laugh. It feels good to laugh with her.

Kylie walks over to the back window and peers out. I can tell she's wondering what's going on with our parents. But it's not like I can tell her. Then she hurries over to the counter, reaches into Mom's purse and pulls out her own cell phone. Mom had taken it away during the movie because Kylie kept texting her friends. She slips her phone into her pocket. "Later," she says, and hurries out of the kitchen.

I glance out the window. They're still out there. Dad has his arm around Mom's shoulders. I take the diary and the other gift back up to my room.

Even though it's barely eight o'clock, I'm exhausted. I bring my parents' gift to bed with me and open it there. Inside a green silk pouch I find eleven gift cards to my favourite stores, each for ten dollars. What a great gift! I place the pouch on my night table, right next to my alarm clock, which I make sure is OFF. I feel more confident tonight than I did last night that Saturday really WILL come. Maybe this was the birthday I was supposed to have, at home with my family.

I start to put SpongeBob in the closet again, but think better of it. I cross the room, push open my window, and toss him out. At first he floats up a foot or two, then the weight of his cardboard hands and feet start to pull him back down. He eventually gets tangled on a tree branch. Leo once used that branch to climb into my room when we were eight and I was grounded for stealing a pack of gum. It was the first and last thing I ever stole. Not including Kylie's diary, which really isn't stealing since I didn't take it out of her room.

"Don't worry," I call out to SpongeBob. "I'll rescue you in the morning."

For the first time in days, I go to bed in a happy mood.

Chapter Ten

When morning comes, it takes the merest glance to see that no balloon rescue will be necessary. SpongeBob is waving happily from the centre of my room, just like he always is. My parents' gift cards are gone from my night table. My mood darkens. I turn off the alarm, and then rip the plug from the wall. I shove the balloon under the bed. I stomp into the bathroom and scrub my face. I stare hopelessly in the mirror. My pupils are so big I can barely see the green around the edges.

Crazy eyes.

Am I crazy? Maybe the whole fight with Leo finally pushed me over the edge and I'm actually locked up in a padded room somewhere, delusional, and unable to move past my eleventh birthday. But even as I think it, I know that's not true. I sit on the edge of the tub, my head in my hands.

"Are you almost done in there?" Kylie asks, pounding on the door.

I open it, and she squeezes past me, wearing the same pink T-shirt she's worn for the past four days. It's almost funny really, since Kylie refuses to wear the same clothes within three weeks of each other. If she only knew!

"You'd better get dressed," she says. "We have to take the bus today."

I grunt and head back to my room. Kylie's door is closed now. It strikes me how differently the same day can go, depending on my choices. I don't feel like going to the doctor again, so I might as well go to school.

I get dressed in my original birthday outfit, and head down for breakfast. Dad's in his robe, drinking his tea. I almost change my mind and go hide under the covers, but he sees me lingering at the door.

"Happy birthday, honey!" he says, sneezing four times in a row.

I grunt.

"Hey, that's no way to be on your birthday. You should be happy today."

I shake the cereal too hard into my bowl and it spills everywhere.

He puts down his newspaper and comes over to me. "Are you OK, Amanda? "

I nod into my bowl, not looking up.

He sneezes a few times, then asks, "Did you like the balloon?"

I don't trust myself to answer so I just nod again. Mom hurries in. "Hi, sweetie," she says, kissing me on my head. "Feel any older?"

I grunt.

"I've gotta run," she says, sticking a granola bar in the pocket of her blazer. "I'll be home early to help you get ready."

I open my mouth to tell her not to bother, that I'm not planning on having the party, but what would my excuse be? I nod miserably instead. She doesn't seem to notice my despair. A minute later Kylie comes in. She grabs her lunch and runs out the door.

Yes! Lunch! Not gonna get me THIS time! I yank my brown bag out of the fridge and stick it in my backpack. I toss in an extra juice box for good measure. I mumble to Dad that I hope he feels better, and run out to the bus stop.

When Kylie continues to ignore me, my bad

mood worsens. I can still remember her laughing with me last night, even if she can't. It almost felt like we were friends. Now it feels like she hates me again. "Just so you know," I say snidely, "he's sitting with her on the bus."

Kylie turns to stare at me. "Who's sitting with who?"

I bite my tongue. What was I thinking? "Never mind."

She leans closer until I can smell her peppermint toothpaste. "Did you read my diary?"

I shake my head, but then figure, what the heck. What could she really do to me? "OK, yes, I read it."

Her eyes narrow at me. "When?"

"Um, this morning?" It was both a lie, and not a lie, at the same time. "You left your door open when you went running."

"But you were in the bathroom the whole time."

OK, that's true. "Trust me, I read it. And don't bother to ask Dustin to the dance, he's gonna say no."

Her expression slackens. I've gone too far. I quickly try to backpedal. "I mean, it's not worth it, he just really likes Alyssa."

Her eyes fill with tears. Clearly that wasn't the right thing to say, either. Fortunately the bus comes before I can make things even worse. When the door opens I step on ahead of Kylie, who is still rooted to the ground. I see the familiar sight of Dustin with his arm around Alyssa and wish I could shield Kylie. But what can I do? I take my usual seat and don't even turn my head when Ruby or Stephanie get on. When we get to school, I let them get off first and wait until I see them go up the school steps before I get off.

"Have a nice day," the bus driver says sweetly. How she can remain calm with thirty screaming kids is beyond me. I notice for the first time that she has a birthmark shaped like a duck on her cheek. It wiggles when she smiles. I don't think she's our usual driver, but I ride so rarely I never paid much attention.

I know I should say thank you, but it comes out as a grunt. I'm NOT going to have a nice day, no matter *who* tells me to. When I get inside, Stephanie and Ruby are in the lobby. When Stephanie sees me, she cuts Ruby off and runs over. Ruby throws me a dirty look.

"Hey, Birthday Girl!" Stephanie says, giving me a hug. I hug her back, but my heart isn't in it.

She walks me to my locker. The streamers and letters look clean and bright again. I mutter something that sounds like a thank you.

"Hey, are you OK?" she asks. "You don't seem like your cheery self."

I force myself to smile. "I'm fine. Just a little worried about tonight. You know, I've never had my own party before."

Stephanie nods and glances down the hall towards Leo's locker. "I know it's weird, but your party will be fun, you'll see. You won't even notice he's not there."

I strain to keep the smile on my face, but it's getting harder. Stephanie gives my arm a final squeeze and runs down to her own locker. "See you at lunch," she calls back.

I turn to my locker, the smile quickly disappearing. Even the colourful sign can't lift my mood. I don't even bother to try my combination. Stopping to readjust my heavy backpack, I notice the lollipop on the floor. Not even looking around, I bend down and grab it. Clutching it tightly, I duck into the classroom. Since I didn't fight with my locker, I'm actually on time today.

Even before the class reads the board and

collectively groans, I'm reaching into my bag for my pen. I don't even bother to glance at Leo, even though I can see out of the corner of my eye that he's in his seat. Maybe if the boy studied once in a while, he wouldn't have to worry so much about failing a pop quiz.

I circle the same answers as before, barely even skimming the questions. I know this test so well I probably could have written it. Jimmy hands me back my 86, and I can't help but turn to look back at Leo. I'm so sure he'll be resting his head in his hands as usual, that it takes me a few seconds to realize that he isn't. What he IS doing is looking directly at ME.

Then he winks.

My heart literally stops. I gape at him for a few seconds before turning to stare down at the desk in front of me. I must have imagined that wink. This isn't the first time that someone has behaved differently from how they did on my first eleventh birthday, but that was only if I did something different first. But this time I did exactly what I did the first time – I glanced at Leo when the test was finished. Then why isn't his head in his hands? I'm afraid to look again. Maybe taking the lollipop messed up the natural order of the universe. Or maybe my timing was off, and he always WOULD have winked at me, if only I'd looked later. For the rest of the class I stare straight ahead, afraid to do or say anything.

"Yes, Mr Fitzpatrick?" Ms Gottlieb says with a few minutes left in the period.

"Can I go to the bathroom?"

My heart starts pounding again. Leo definitely did not ask for a hall pass before.

Ms Gottlieb sighs. "I'm sure you CAN, Leo."

The class snickers. Leo corrects himself. "I mean, MAY I go to the bathroom?"

Ms Gottlieb glances at the clock. "Can it wait till the end of class?"

I turn around in time to see Leo shaking his head.

Another sigh as she fishes the hall pass from her drawer. "You might as well bring your things with you and return this after your next class."

As Leo makes his way down the aisle towards me, I slide further down in my chair. I'm so used to knowing what's going to happen next, that at first I don't realize that something has just landed on my desk with a gentle *plop*. I watch the door close behind Leo. Slowly my eyes focus on the folded piece of notebook paper sitting in the middle of my open history book. I tentatively reach for it, afraid to even guess what it says. Ms Gottlieb is giving out the homework assignment, but since I already know what it is, I bring the note down to my lap and fumble until it's open. It has been a year since I've seen Leo's handwriting, but it's as familiar to me as my own.

AMANDA,

MEET ME OUTSIDE THE CAF AT LUNCH TIME. OH, AND HAPPY BIRTHDAY! (For the fourth time!)

LEO

My arms fly up of their own accord and knock my backpack to the floor with a big crash. I have to cling on to the sides of my desk so I don't fall off my chair.

"Is there a problem, Miss Ellerby?" Ms Gottlieb asks wearily.

I don't trust myself to speak, so I shake my head and scramble to pick up my books. I'm still on the floor when the bell rings. My classmates file past me. I sit back on my heels, and shove the note deep into my pocket. Just when I was sure I knew the rules to this whole "day-repeating-thing," it's like the rules are changing. Leo could only mean one thing when he wrote "for the fourth time." He knows what's going on. But how? Was it something I did that, like, woke him up? Or has he known from the beginning? If he did know, he's been pretty good at hiding it. I guess I'll have to meet him to find out. But it's been a year since I've spoken to him, and now I'm just supposed to pretend nothing happened?

The rest of the morning is a blur. I don't even bother stopping at the office to request that my locker be fixed. As soon as Leo sees me approach the cafeteria, he motions for me to follow him back down the hall. My friends are going to wonder where I am when I don't show up at lunch, but I have to do this.

Leo leads me to the end of the hall and pushes open the door to the courtyard that only the gardening class uses. I stop, but he grabs my arm and pulls me outside, letting the door swing closed behind me. Neither of us speak. It feels so strange being here with him. Over the past year I've imagined how our first conversation would go a million times, and it usually started with him on his knees begging for forgiveness. He's not on his knees now, though.

He breaks the silence. "So, um, how's it going?"

In light of everything that's happened over the past four days, I can't even BEGIN to answer that question. I look him straight in the face and do the last thing I ever thought I would if this day came. I burst out laughing.

"How's it going?" I repeat. I keep laughing until my sides ache and I have to wrap my arms around myself. His face lights up. He starts laughing, too, and soon we're kneeling on the cobblestones, clutching our sides and gasping for breath. I collect myself first.

"I still . . . hate you," I say in between gulps of air.

He nods, trying to get control of himself. "I know. But I think . . . that we . . . we. . ." He starts cracking up again, then forces himself to stop. "I think we have bigger problems right now."

"We sure do!" I wipe at my eyes. We both lean back on our heels. "But I'm confused about something. Every time I saw you on the second day, you were doing the same things you had done on the first day. Like everyone else."

"So were you," he points out. "I figured I was alone in this. And then yesterday when you didn't show up for the quiz, I couldn't believe it. I wanted to call you, but I was too freaked out. Then when I winked at you and you made that face, I knew."

"What face?" I ask, getting defensive.

"It was like you saw a ghost."

I cross my arms, annoyed. "Well, you would have reacted the same way."

"Believe me, I'm sure I looked like that when that pop quiz started and you weren't in your chair. Look, you and I seem to be the only people this is happening to, so there's no sense arguing."

"But why us?"

"I've been trying to figure that out, but I can't."

I look at my watch. "We better get back in there. Stephanie's going to start looking for me."

"You're right. We don't want to draw any attention to ourselves." He gathers his books and stands up. "And I don't think we should let people see us together. It'd be too hard to explain why we're suddenly friends."

I stiffen. All the hurt from his mean words comes flooding back. "We're *not* friends," I say coldly, swinging my bag over my shoulder.

"Well, you know what I mean," Leo says, shifting his weight from foot to foot.

I take a bit of pity on him and ask, "So what do we do now?"

"I think we should lie low," he says hurriedly, "and do everything as close as possible to the way we did it the first time. Then after our parties I'll sneak over and we can compare notes. You know, about everything we've been through these last few days. Maybe together we can figure out what's going on."

The thought of going through with my party again makes me want to hide under a rock. I'm sure *his* party was great so it's not much of a hardship for him. We don't speak as we head back inside. Leo clears his throat as we approach the cafeteria. "Um, just so you know, I've felt horrible every day for what I said at our party last year. I didn't mean any of it."

Unable to meet his eyes I ask, "Then why'd you say it?"

"It's a long story. Any chance we can just skip it and be friends again?"

I shake my head.

"I didn't think so. I'll explain tonight, I promise."

I turn to go, but he reaches out and stops me. "Amanda? Thank you."

"For what?"

"For reading my note and for meeting me. I was really scared you wouldn't. I just . . . I. . ."

I look up to see his eyes fill with tears. For the first time it occurs to me that maybe it wasn't allergies that made his face red and blotchy those other days. I want to ask him why he was in the guidance counsellor's office. I want to ask him a million things. But for now I just nod.

We stand there awkwardly. I glance down at my watch, then grab a surprised Leo by the sleeve and push him out of the way. A second later the crying Bee Boy throws open his classroom door and flies into the hall. A second earlier and the door would have crashed right into Leo's head.

"Wow, thanks!" Leo says, eyes wide.

"No problem." I turn and quickly walk towards the cafeteria.

I can tell, even without turning around, that Leo is smiling.

Chapter Eleven

Humiliating myself in gymnastics tryouts is easier to handle this time. One good thing about being stuck doing this with Leo is that I can cross off "I'm going crazy" from my list of reasons why this is happening. I don't think people go crazy together.

When it comes time to put on my costume, I've thought of a few ways to make it less horrible. I slip on a T-shirt first so the lace isn't as itchy, and put fresh Band-Aids on my ankles so the shoes don't hurt as much. When I come out of the bathroom, Kylie's door is still closed. I haven't seen her since I've been home, which works out fine for me. The warning on the cover of her diary was probably just a bluff, but I don't want to take any chances. I'm about to head downstairs to greet the first arrivals when her door swings open, making me jump. She's still wearing the clothes she wore to school.

"Where's your costume?"

"I'm not wearing one."

I knew she'd be mad, but I didn't expect her not to dress up for my party. "But you looked so great in it."

She puts her hands on her hips. "How do you know how I looked in it? Are you spying on me now?"

I've said the wrong thing again. "I mean, I'm SURE you'd look great in it."

"Well, I'm not wearing it. Thanks to you, this has been a really awful day."

I'm taken aback. "Me? Why?"

"You know why. All that stuff you said about Dustin liking Alyssa instead of me."

"Er, but isn't that true?"

She glares and I back up a step. "I'll never know because I didn't ask him to the dance and now he's going with her."

"But he was always going with her, right?" Clearly the rules of teenage dating rituals are something I have yet to figure out.

"And then if that wasn't enough," she

continues, ignoring my last question, "I forgot my science project and my teacher took off half a grade and Dustin's really mad at me."

"But that wasn't your fault," I insist. "Mom took your poster by mistake. Maybe if she calls your teacher and explains—"

For the first time today, Kylie's lips curl up into something resembling a smile. It's the kind of smile you see on the Nature Channel before one seemingly harmless animal devours another. She stomps back into her room and slams the door shut.

I knock. "Aren't you coming to my party?"

No answer. I guess this is how she's getting back at me for reading her diary.

Seeing as I know what to expect, I'm not disappointed this time that so many people don't show up. I try to make the party more fun for the people who did come. We play silly kids' games like limbo and musical chairs. Dad sneezes into the punch bowl by mistake, and everyone laughs (then Mom takes away the punch bowl). I'm still thinking of Leo's party, and wondering how it's going, but this time it's different. This time I know for sure that he's thinking of me, too.

When everyone leaves I don't wait for Mom's

news. I take the stairs two at a time to get ready for Leo's visit. I'm so curious to hear what his experiences have been like that I can hardly sit still. My costume rips as I pull it off and at first I feel bad since it's rented. Then I realize it'll just fix itself tomorrow! At this point I'd be more surprised if Saturday DOES come than if it doesn't.

I wait by the window for Leo, figuring he'll probably climb up the branch instead of ringing the bell. I'm sure he doesn't want to deal with anyone in my family answering the door. I wouldn't blame him. He's not exactly Mr Popularity around here.

My door bangs open and I jump. We have a knocking rule in our house and someone has just broken it. I turn around expecting to see Kylie, but instead it's Mom, her face red. She's carrying a poster under her arm. Usually this is when she'd be telling me about losing her job, but tonight she looks angry. Maybe I should have stayed to help clean up. Before I have a chance to apologize, she says in an even tone, "I know this was a hard day for you. For the first time in your life you didn't celebrate your birthday with Leo. You normally make such good choices and have proven you know right from wrong. All that said, I can't imagine why you wanted to sabotage my job."

My eyes widen and I search my brain for what she could possibly be talking about. "Huh? What?"

She hands me the poster and gestures for me to unroll it. It's her presentation. "Maybe you'd like to explain to me how this wound up in the outside garbage?"

"What? Why was it in the garbage?"

"That's what I'd like YOU to tell ME."

"But how would I know?"

"Your sister told me you knew I had her poster with me at work. There's no way you could have known about it if you hadn't switched them. No one knew except my clients. And my boss, of course, who fired me a few minutes ago."

I sink down on to the corner of my bed. How was I going to get out of this one? I couldn't exactly tell her that I knew because she told me. Three times!

"OK, Amanda, you don't have to tell me. Birthday or no birthday, you're grounded until you can tell me the truth. I don't have to tell you how disappointed I am."

She grabs her poster and leaves my door wide open when she storms out. Kylie peeks her head out of her own room and gives me a wide smile. *Grrr!* So THIS is how she's getting me back. I guess I should have taken the warning on her diary a little more seriously!

Fuming, I sit by the window again. Wait till Leo hears about THIS one. I'm still waiting, tracing my breath on the window, when the doorbell rings. I hear Mom clomp over to it and I step into the hall to hear better.

"Um, hi, Mrs Ellerby. I came over to talk to Amanda."

There's a pause – probably from shock – and then Mom says, "Amanda is grounded until further notice."

"But—"

"No buts, Leo. And you have a lot of nerve coming here. We've missed you a lot this past year, you know."

I can practically see him staring down at his feet. He always does that when he's embarrassed. "I missed you all, too," he says, although I can barely make out the words.

Then the door closes with a definite finality. Why oh why did he choose the door instead of the window? I'm about to cross back over to the window when I hear the front door open again. Mom shouts out, "And don't try climbing that tree! Grounded means grounded!"

I run over to the window in time to see Leo pedalling away on his bike. I can't believe that after waiting all day, I'm not going to talk to Leo tonight. I put on my pyjamas and climb into bed. I can feel the frustration rising up in me. Grounded for something I didn't do! What a horrible fate! I want to scream that I didn't do it, that Kylie is setting me up.

But a smile slowly spreads across my face as I stare up at the ceiling. What am I getting so worked up over? In a few hours no one will remember any of this except for me and Leo. For the first time, I can't wait to see SpongeBob's freaky streamer arms waving at me in the morning.

Chapter Twelve

And there he is! Waving and smiling, just like always. I jump up and hug him. Mom and Kylie don't hate me any more, and Leo and I are in this together! Woo-hoo!

Then it hits me – I forgot to hide the balloon last night! Maybe it really ISN'T still my birthday. I look wildly around my room and grab at the Dorothy costume. I turn it around in my hands until I find where the rip should be, right at the seam of the underarm. I feel all around, but it's perfectly fine! Woo-hoo, again!

I get dressed and run downstairs. I hesitate for a second at the entrance to the kitchen, where I can see Dad at the counter with his tea. I couldn't still be grounded, could I?

"Um, hi Dad," I say cautiously. I step back a bit

in preparation for the four sneezes that have greeted me each morning.

"Hi, honey!" he says, and then sneezes on schedule. "Happy birthday!"

I release my breath. All clear. "Thanks! And thanks for the balloon."

Before he can tell me that Kylie thought I was too old for it, Mom rushes in. "Hi, sweetie," she says, bending to kiss my forehead. "Feel any older?"

I give her a big hug. She's not mad at me any more! "I do, I feel a lot older. Like I turned eleven five days ago!"

She laughs and points to the birthday cake in the plastic box on the counter. "Well, I'm pretty sure if you turned eleven five days ago we'd have eaten that cake by now!"

I want to tell her that we HAVE eaten it, many times, and that it could have used more Oreo crumbles on top, but instead I just smile and pour my bowl of cereal. "Good luck on the presentation!"

"Thanks," she says, grabbing her granola bar, "I'll need it. I'm sorry you have to take the bus today, but I've really gotta run."

I turn back to my cereal and then, with a sharp

intake of breath, I drop my spoon. It lands in the bowl with a splash that sends milk spraying into my face. "Mom, wait!"

She stops halfway out the door. "What is it, Amanda? I can't be late."

I jump up and pull the poster from under her arm. "This isn't your presentation. It's Kylie's science project." I slide off the rubber band and hold it up. Sure enough, it's a diagram on how a solid becomes a liquid and then a gas.

Her eyes widen when she sees it. "I must have left mine upstairs!" She drops her overflowing briefcase to the floor. "How did you know?"

Good question. "Um, I saw her leave it here last night?"

She gives me a hug. "You better hurry and finish your breakfast before the bus comes." She rushes out of the kitchen just as Kylie rushes in. Kylie barely has time to step out of the way. "Don't forget your poster," Mom says as she passes.

"That's where that is!" Kylie says, rolling it back up. I half expect her to thank me but, of course, she doesn't know the trouble I just saved her. She tucks it under her arm, waves goodbye to Dad, and runs out the back door. Hmm.

Interesting. She forgot her lunch. I guess the thing with the poster distracted her from what she would normally have done. I gulp down my juice and then grab both our lunches.

"Bye, Dad! Feel better."

"Not so fast," he says, then coughs a few times. "I know for a fact Kylie didn't leave that poster in here last night. She left it on the coffee table in the den. I brought it in this morning."

I feel my cheeks grow hot. "Oh?"

"Not that it really matters. A good deed is a good deed."

"Right! Gotta go."

"I've got my eye on you," he says playfully, wagging his finger.

"Er, OK, Dad! Bye!" I run out before I manage to mess up again. When I reach the bus stop I hand Kylie her lunch. Now that I know what depths of meanness she's capable of when crossed, it pays to stay on her good side. Even if she won't remember it tomorrow.

"Thanks," she mutters, stuffing the paper bag into her backpack.

We stand in silence. If I didn't know her brain was consumed with thoughts of Dustin and the dance, I'd be annoyed that she's still not wishing me a happy birthday. But when I think about it, on that first birthday she had lost the guy, lost half her grade in science and still got dressed up for my party. That must mean she doesn't totally hate me. The bus pulls up and as the doors open, I wish I could find a way to shield her from seeing Dustin with his arm around Alyssa. But nothing comes to me that wouldn't lead to her figuring out I read her diary.

And I know how *that* ends.

I want to share my good mood with someone other than an empty seat. So when Stephanie gets on, I stand up and wave so she can't help but see me. She smiles and then glances quickly at Ruby, who glares at me. I wonder fleetingly if Stephanie is still going to choose Ruby over me. She doesn't. And even though she spends the whole ride talking about gymnastics and the fun things we'll do when we're best friends with Mena and Heather and Jess, I'm still happy that she chose me. Especially since I know that once she makes the team and I don't, that won't be the case.

When we get to my locker, I'm about to thank her for decorating it when she says, "Wow, that looks great! Who did it?"

I crinkle my brows. "What do you mean? YOU did it!"

She shakes her head. "No, I didn't."

"But you told me you did."

"Huh? I swear, I didn't decorate your locker. If you'd like me to take credit for it though, I'm happy to."

This is very weird. Why would she have lied about such a small thing? And it's not like I can ask her since she obviously doesn't remember lying about it. "But if you didn't do it, who did?"

"I did," a voice from behind says.

We both whirl around and find ourselves face-to-face with Leo. He's smiling.

"YOU did this?" Stephanie and I say at the same time.

His smile broadens. "Yup. I came in early this morning." I stare at him, truly shocked.

"Um, I'm going to leave you two alone," Stephanie says, backing away. "Looks like you have a lot to talk about." She hurries down the hall, glancing backwards at us every few feet.

I pull Leo into an empty classroom. "You've been decorating my locker every day?"

He nods. "It was easy. I had already cut out all the letters the night before our birthday, so each morning when I woke up, they were in my backpack ready to be taped on your locker."

"But why would Stephanie take credit for it every other day, but not today?"

"Because she felt bad that you had to sit alone on the bus," he explains. "Then you were so happy when you thought she decorated it, she just couldn't correct you. But I bet you sat together today, so she had no reason to take credit for the locker."

I narrow my eyes at him. "How do you know all that?"

"Well, um, I was sort of lurking nearby to see your reaction that first day. I thought you'd be so happy about the locker that you'd listen to my apology about, you know, last year. Then Stephanie jumped in and took the credit. I overheard her tell the story to Emma in math."

"So if you knew all that, why didn't you tell me the truth?"

He shrugs. "Stephanie's been your friend all year, while I . . . well, you know. So I figure she deserved to have her secret kept."

That was really decent of him. I look at Leo closely for the first time in a year. He's taller, by a few inches. He's wearing his dark hair a little shorter. I wonder how else he's changed. If I hadn't got grounded last night, I would have found out. Kids start streaming into the class and we slip back out to the hall.

"Why were you grounded last night?" he asks. "I left my party before it was over because I couldn't wait to come over."

"After having your party four times, something tells me you weren't too broken up about leaving early."

He smiles. "True."

"Basically I got grounded because I snuck into Kylie's room and read her diary. It actually told me some interesting things, but then she found out and set me up. My mom was furious. But hey, my parents don't remember I got grounded, Kylie doesn't remember about the diary, and I still remember everything I read in it. So it all worked out."

Leo is nodding thoughtfully. "Remind me to tell you my thoughts on consequences."

"We have a lot to talk about first," I say, noticing for the first time that kids who pass by are staring at us. Our friendship break-up was kind of legendary. Leo must have noticed, too, because he drops his voice.

"Meet me in the courtyard after first period."

I shake my head and whisper, "I have maths."

"Skip it," he urges. "It's not like it'll matter tomorrow."

He has a point. "But what if today is the last time this happens and tomorrow really IS tomorrow?"

"Then we'll have all weekend to come up with a reason why we skipped second period."

"OK." We run into our history class just as the late bell rings. Needless to say, we both ace the pop quiz.

Chapter Thirteen

I'm about to leave the courtyard and go to maths class when Leo finally arrives. "What took you so long?"

"The guidance counsellor seriously has it in for me," he says, plopping down on the grass next to me. "I went into her office to cancel our meeting for this afternoon and she made me sit and talk to her. I told her I was gonna be late for English, and she gave me this." He holds up a blue pass. "Looks like you're the only one actually cutting class!"

I snatch the paper from his hand and pretend to rip it up. He grabs for it, then says, "Go ahead. We're in this together."

I smooth it out and hand it back. "That's OK. Keep it." I want to ask him why he was seeing the guidance counsellor in the first place, but there's something else I want to know even more. Twining a strand of grass around my finger, I ask, "Why did you say those things?" and brace myself for his answer.

He doesn't insult me by asking *what things*, which is really good because then I might have left. "I tried to explain last year." He yanks up his own pieces of grass, shredding them as he goes. "But you wouldn't listen to me."

"I didn't want to be in the same room as you."

"Look, I don't blame you. What I said was horrible, but you've got to know I didn't mean it. What can I do to make it up to you?"

I think about that for a minute. "If I come up with something big enough, I'll let you know."

"Listen, Amanda, you're my, I mean you were my best friend for my whole life. I don't even remember a time that you weren't right there next to me, since I was born. You were, you know, like my sister. And sometimes brothers say really mean things about their sisters, you know, to sound cool in front of their friends."

"But I'm NOT your sister!" The grass is wrapped so tight around my finger that the tip is turning purple.

"Duh, I know that. I knew right as it came out of my mouth that night that I shouldn't have said those things. I know you have lots of friends other than me. I'm sure your party this year was great."

I open my mouth and then quickly think better of it. He doesn't need to know that only eight people showed up and that even Stephanie left in the middle. "And the part about not wanting to share our birthdays any more? Did you really mean that?"

He shakes his head and looks miserable. "Of course not. I had a terrible time at my party – I mean *parties* – this year. It just wasn't the same."

I have to admit I feel a little shiver of pleasure hearing that he didn't have fun at his party. But mostly I feel relieved that he hadn't meant the things he said. "I still don't understand why you said that stuff in the first place. Why would you pick those guys over me? Everyone knows how obnoxious they are."

He squirms a little. "I can't really explain it. They were hanging out in my room and those guys never wanted to hang out with me before. I didn't want them to think my best friend was a girl."

"But why would they care? What's the

difference if I'm a boy or a girl?"

He shrugs. "They think girls just sit around and have tea parties and play with stuffed animals."

"What am I, five?"

He holds up his hands. "Hey, I don't think that. I'm just telling you what they said."

"Well, why didn't you come after me when I left the party?"

"I couldn't. I was too embarrassed. And then when my mom found out what happened, she was so mad at me she gave me the cold shoulder for a week. She said you were like the daughter she always wanted and wasn't able to have. She asks me about you all the time, but I can't even tell her anything. She misses you."

My eyes sting with tears. "I miss her, too. And I miss..." I can't bring myself to say "I miss YOU" but I think he knows because he holds out his hand and says, "Friends again?"

I take it and we shake. "Friends." Then we feel silly and quickly snatch our hands away. I glance at the door to the courtyard, just to make sure no one saw us. Still shut tight. OK, first order of business down. Time for the next. "So, what was your reaction when you woke up that first time and realized it was our birthday again?"

"I thought it was a joke!" I laugh. "Me too!"

"The first thing I heard when I woke up was my mom playing the guitar while my Dad sang 'Happy Birthday' to me. I was like, *Very funny guys, my birthday was yesterday*. But they just kept strumming and singing, and the phone rang and it was the football guy – who calls himself *Paul the Ball* – confirming the party and before I knew it, we had that pop quiz again. I felt like a zombie, just going through the motions, scared to do anything differently from the day before."

"Me too!"

He continues. "I really, really wanted to tell you what was going on but I couldn't. I figured you'd never believe me. Plus, you know, you hadn't spoken to me in a year."

"Yeah, there's that."

"So I told myself it was all a bad dream, but when it happened again on the third day, I started to get really scared. I seriously thought I was going crazy. Then you weren't in school and it was like fireworks went off in my head. I knew that this had to be happening to you, too, or else you'd be sitting in that class with me. And I finally knew I wasn't dreaming, I wasn't crazy.

What was it like for you?"

I take a deep breath and tell him everything that happened. He laughs when I get to the part about swinging my arms pathetically at gymnastics tryouts. He mumbles "Sorry" when I tell him that Stephanie left to go to his party. I show him my healing blisters and explain that they're the reason I knew this was real. I tell him about Kylie and what I read in her diary, and about Mom getting fired.

When I'm done he leans forward intently and says, "We're like, we're . . . special or something. Like time is stopping for us."

"But why? Why us? Is it something we did? Something we *didn't* do? Maybe everyone's stuck, but only the two of us realize it. Or maybe there are others, but we don't know about them and they don't know about us."

"I hadn't thought about others," he says, sitting back on his heels. "I guess it's possible. We should find out."

"Don't you think our first job should be to make it stop?"

"Who says we should make it stop?" He smiles crookedly, the old sparkle back in his eye. I missed that sparkle. Leo was definitely the leader when it came to anything sneaky.

"What do you mean?"

He jumps up. "Think about it. You know how our parents – well, mostly *your* parents – are always saying that there are 'consequences for our actions'?" He does a pretty good imitation of my dad.

"Yeah, so?"

"Well, that rule doesn't apply to us any more. We can do anything we want and the slate is wiped clean the next day."

"What slate?"

"It's an *expression*," he says, still excited. "It's like we get a 'do-over' every day!"

I think back to this morning, and how happy I was that no one in my family remembered they were mad at me. I begin to see where he's going with this. "Do you have a plan?"

He can barely contain himself and actually does a little hop and a skip. Good thing those guys he was trying so hard to impress can't see him now. "I have a few ideas," he says. "I want to check some things out first."

I shiver involuntarily. "Is it going to get us in trouble?"

"There's a good chance," he admits.

The bell rings. "Should we go back to class? Those consequences you talked about might be gone tomorrow, but if we cut school we'll still get in a lot of trouble today. I can't stand my parents being mad at me again, even if it just lasts a day. And if we get grounded, we can't do anything anyway."

"You're right." He picks up his backpack and hands me mine. "We should start tomorrow. That'll give me more time to plan anyway. If you pretend you're sick again, can you get out of the house without being seen?"

"I think so. My dad pretty much slept all day. He'll just think I'm sleeping, too." I push open the door to the hallway and we quickly blend in with the streams of kids coming out of classrooms.

"I'll go to school like usual," Leo says, raising his voice over the commotion. "But I'll hand in a note saying I have a doctor's appointment and won't be back."

"Isn't that risky?"

"I don't have a choice. If I just cut, the school will call to find out where I am. My parents will be home all day, getting ready for my party, so they'd definitely answer the phone."

"I guess having a hypnotist, a famous football

player, a live band, and a giant lizard *would* take a lot of preparation."

He winces. "Well, if it makes you feel any better, the rock band sent a replacement. Every night I've had to listen to Hop-along Willie and the Knee-slapping Five."

I stifle a laugh. "What kind of band is *that*?"

He shudders. "You don't want to know. And the giant lizard? Just a regular lizard with a weight problem. Believe me, I didn't ask for my party to be this big deal. My parents did it because they knew how hard this was on me. You know, having my party alone. So really, it's all *your* fault."

"Well, if it makes you feel any better," I tell him as we reach the end of the hall, "you don't have to decorate my locker tomorrow."

He pretends to pout. "But then no one will see how creative I am."

The warning bell rings for the next period. I only have a minute now to get all the way across the school. "I've gotta run, so I'll see you tomorrow morning. And this time, use the branch, will ya?" I turn to go and discover a little crowd has formed a few feet away from us. A few of the kids are whispering and glancing our way.

"I guess our secret's out," Leo says. "People

know we made up."

"But they don't know our *real* secret," I whisper.

"That's true. And by tomorrow, they'll forget they saw us!"

We give each other a high five and a wave to the crowd before going our separate ways. Leo was right. This could actually be fun!

Chapter Fourteen

I switch off my alarm and stare up at the dark ceiling. I can barely make out the flowers painted on it. I can't wait to tell Leo what happened last night – Mom still got fired! Even though I had given her the right poster! I couldn't believe it when she told me. When I asked why they were firing her, she just shrugged and said her boss didn't think she was "a good fit" for the company any more.

Mom comes in to see why I'm not up, and I give my story about being sick. Everything is going according to plan until she sighs and says, "Mrs Grayson down the street will have to take you to the doctor."

Ugh! How could I have forgotten about this part? My mind races for some way to get out of it, but nothing comes. I nod weakly. Once she leaves, I wait a little while until I hear her car start in the driveway, followed quickly by Kylie slamming the back door. The less I have to talk to anyone, the less chance I have for messing up. It feels weird letting them go without telling them about the poster switcheroo, but since it didn't do any good – Mom's still gonna get fired, and Kylie's still not gonna get the guy – I might as well not bother.

So what to do about the doctor? Maybe Leo can call my dad, pretending to be from the doctor's office. He can say the doctor had an emergency and can I come in tomorrow? Or maybe I'll call Mrs Grayson and pretend to be Mom and tell her I don't have to go after all. I really hate lying. Consequences or no, it doesn't make me feel good.

When I don't go downstairs for breakfast, Dad knocks on my door. "Come in," I call out weakly.

The door opens and he walks in with a tall glass of orange juice and a muffin. He places them on my night table. "Happy birthday, sweetie! You must really not be feeling well if you're still in bed."

I nod and glance out the window. "I'm going to be in bed a lot today."

When I look back, I see him sizing me up with his eyes. Then he says, "I know this is a hard day for you. But you didn't cancel your party tonight so you don't have to compete with Leo's, right?"

Normally I would argue that this isn't about Leo, but what do you know? It actually IS! But I shake my head and cough a few times. "I just don't feel well, Dad."

"OK," he says, backing away and sneezing. "I'll be on the couch downstairs if you need anything. I'll come get you when Mrs Grayson gets here."

As he closes the door it occurs to me that I might not have to go to such elaborate lengths to get out of going to the doctor. Maybe all I have to do is appeal to Dad's soft-hearted nature. "Wait, Dad?" I call out.

He comes back in. "That was fast."

Now that he's here I'm not sure what to say. "Um, can I just ask one small favour?"

"Sure, honey. It is your birthday after all."

That's it! I can work with that! "Yes, right, it's my birthday, and well, it'd be really awful if I had to go to the doctor on my birthday. I mean, it's bad enough that I have to cancel my party and everything. . . Is there any way I can go to the doctor tomorrow, instead? I'm sure I have what you have, you know, just a cold."

"Hmm, it is Friday, so you'd have the whole weekend to recover."

I hold my breath while he considers. This definitely isn't the right time to tell him weekends don't seem to exist for me lately. Finally he says, "OK, I guess it's a reasonable request. I'll tell the doctor we'll call tomorrow if you don't feel any better."

I want to jump up and give him a hug, but I still need to be sick enough to spend the day in bed. "Thanks, Dad!"

"OK, OK." He smiles and heads for the door. "I won't bother you, just come get me if you need anything. Try to get some sleep. That's what I plan to do."

"I will," I say, crossing my fingers under the covers.

I stay in bed until I hear his footfalls on the stairs, then push aside the breakfast he brought me and throw on my clothes. I wrench open the bottom of my tooth-shaped piggy bank and pull out the crumpled bills I've stashed in there over the years, compliments of the tooth fairy. Smoothing everything out on the bed, I count exactly forty-two dollars. That's a lot of teeth! I don't know what Leo has planned, but it never hurts to be prepared.

I've just placed the piggy bank back on the shelf when I hear a knock on the window. Leo's grinning face is framed in the glass. I hurry to open the window, and Leo swings one leg over the windowsill and almost falls on to the floor.

Picking leaves off his shirt he says, "Either that tree has got smaller or I've got bigger. Didn't you hear the branch crack? I thought I was a goner."

I shake my head, glancing out at the tree. It doesn't look any different to me.

"We'll have to go out a different way," he says. Then he sees the money spread out on my bed. "How much you got? I stopped at the bank and wiped out my savings account."

"You *did?*"

He nods, the old sparkle back again. "I figured, why not? It'll just replace itself tomorrow!"

"Good thinking! So how much do you have?"

He holds up a wad of cash. "Three hundred dollars!"

"Wow!" I've never seen that much money before. I reach out to touch it.

"So how much do you have?" he repeats.

"Um, forty-two." Suddenly it doesn't seem as impressive. He gathers it up and adds it to his stack. "That's OK, we have plenty."

"Wait a sec! I do have more! Well, it's not cash, but my parents gave me gift cards for my birthday."

"Great!" he says. "Where are they?"

I turn towards the night table and stop. "Oh, right, they're gone now. Never mind." I slip on my sneakers and turn to the door.

But Leo doesn't move. "Does your mom still hide your presents under her bed?"

"I guess so, but if we take them, they'll find out tonight."

He shakes his head. "Not if you don't open your gifts tonight."

He's right! I've only opened the gifts once since this started happening. I'll just put it off again.

Five minutes later we're out the back door, gift cards securely in hand. Dad hadn't even twitched when we snuck past him. Still, we keep tiptoeing until we're two houses down.

"Close your eyes," Leo says. "I'll be back in a second." So I stand on the sidewalk, eyes closed.

Just as I'm starting to feel stupid, he says, "OK, open them."

He's holding on to the handlebars of two electric scooters. He grins and hands me a pink helmet. He plops a silver one on his head, and clicks the buckle closed. "Fully charged and ready to go. What do you think?"

"I think you stole these from the Schwartz's garage across the street!"

He shakes his head. "I *borrowed* them, there's a difference. I fully intend to bring them back before they even notice they're missing."

I'm not convinced.

"Amanda, if this day is going to work at all, you're gonna have to go with it. I know we'd never do stuff like this normally. But nothing's normal now, remember?"

He's right, of course. For one day I can let go a little. Leo would never say it, but I can be as uptight as my mom. I climb on to my scooter, and strap on my helmet. "What are we waiting for, then?"

He grins and hops on his own. "Follow me," he says, and takes off down the block.

We wind in and out of the streets until we approach the centre of town. I love the feeling of the warm breeze on my face and am sorry when Leo pulls up in front of the diner. I pull up next to him and switch off the motor.

"First stop," he says, running his hands through his helmet-matted hair. "Breakfast!"

I think of the untouched juice and muffin and my stomach growls. We leave the scooters outside and find a booth by the window so we can watch them while we eat. Not that there's much crime in Willow Falls, but still, they're not ours to lose.

When the waitress comes, Leo orders pancakes with chocolate chips and strawberries, an omelette with sausage and peppers, French toast with powdered sugar and pecans, hot chocolate with whipped cream, orange juice, home fries, regular fries with gravy and a bowl of chocolate pudding. "I'll just share his," I tell her, shaking my head in wonderment.

"School off today or something?" she asks, reaching for our menus.

Leo and I glance at each other. We hadn't talked about what to do if someone asked us this. Leo must have thought about it, though, because he quickly says, "We won a contest so we get to come in late."

I cringe and sink a little in my seat. A contest? That's the best he could come up with?

"Good for you," she says genuinely. "Only thing I ever won was a turkey at a Thanksgiving parade. Pulled my back out lifting it and was in bed for a week." She heads towards the kitchen, shaking her head.

"A *contest?*" I whisper.

"Sure, why not?"

"What kind of contest did we win, exactly?"

Leo pauses to take a sip of his water. "Don't you remember? We guessed the amount of jelly beans in the fishbowl."

"That was in second grade!"

"Hey, I never told her *when* we won the contest!"

I have to admit that's true. After a glance to make sure our scooters are still there, I ask Leo, "So, what are we going to do today?"

"The question is, what *aren't* we going to do?"

A tingle of anticipation and nerves run through me. "Really?"

He shakes his head. "Nah. We live in the most boring town in the world. I've just always wanted to say that."

The waitress brings the juice and hot chocolate,

along with two extra glasses. Being with Leo now makes me realize I never should have let a whole year go by. That's 1/11th of my life that we missed spending together. My maths teacher would be proud of my fractioning ability.

The waitress sets down the plates, and they cover most of the table. She turns to go when Leo stops her. "Ma'am?" he says. My heart sinks. Why can't he leave well enough alone?

"Yeah?"

"I know this sounds strange, but what day is it today?"

"It's Friday," she says tiredly. "The end of a long week."

"So if today's Friday," he says, "what was yesterday?"

Now she's starting to look irritated. "What do you mean what was yesterday? Yesterday was Thursday."

"You're sure?" Leo asks. "You don't need to think about it?"

In response she slaps the bill down on the table and says, "Maybe you should hurry off to school. You need some learning in you if you don't know the days of the week at your age!"

I glare at him. "Why, Leo, why?"

His mouth already full of pancake, he says, "You said we need to ask people if every day is Friday for them, too. I figured why not start with her?"

"Because she can report us for cutting school."

He points his fork at the omelette. "You're gonna want to try this. It's delicious."

I sigh, and reach over for a piece. "At least with your mouth full you're less likely to get us in trouble."

We plough through breakfast like we've never eaten before. We've certainly never eaten like THIS before. About halfway through, my stomach lurches. I push the plates towards Leo.

As he opens his mouth to shovel in more pancakes, I gasp. He drops his fork with a clang against the side of his plate. "What is it?"

"I just remembered — when I stayed home last time Stephanie called! I should have called her this morning before school to let her know I wasn't coming. Now my dad's gonna get the phone and come up to my room!"

"What time did she call?"

I shake my head. "I'm not sure. Soon, though. Probably between second and third period?"

"OK, let's not panic," he says, picking up the check the waitress had left on the table. He peels some bills off our stack and tucks them under the check. Usually we'd be scrounging for quarters to pay for French fries. He sticks one more forkful in his mouth, then grabs both our helmets and slides out of the booth. I'm not sure if my stomach hurts from all the food or from the thought that my dad might go upstairs and find an empty bed.

"OK, I think I've got it," he says once we're back at the scooters. "Where's Stephanie during second period?"

I pause to think. "Gym class, I think."

He looks at his watch. I recognize it as the one he got for our ninth birthday. It's waterproof and apparently can tell time on the moon. "We have about twenty minutes before the end of second period. If we can get to the school on time, we can find her out on the field. C'mon, let's go."

Before I have a chance to ask questions about this plan, Leo's halfway down the block. I hop on and take off after him. The scooter doesn't go very fast, and it's a little tricky staying on the sidewalks, but it's pretty fun. I can't believe we're actually going to school and cutting school at the same time. I wouldn't have thought that was possible. What if someone looks out the window and recognizes us? Leo must be thinking the same thing, because he makes a wide circle around the school, pulling up as close to the back field as possible. A group of kids in yellow-and-green gym outfits are jogging towards the back door, kicking a ball back and forth. I spot Stephanie walking next to Tracy. They're close enough that their words float back to me. They're arguing whether a hot dog counts as meat or some yet-to-be-discovered substance. Tracy wouldn't eat a hot dog if her life depended on it. Not that I can imagine a situation where someone's life would hinge on a hot dog, except maybe one of those reality shows where you have to eat weird things or else you're voted off. Why am I thinking of hot dogs at a time like this?

I turn off my scooter and run to Leo's side. "They're starting to go in! What should we do?"

Leo whips off his helmet and hands it to me. "I'll take care of it," he says. "Just stay low."

He races off toward the back door of the gym and I duck behind a bush. My heart racing, I peek out as far as I dare. I'm just in time to see Leo pull Stephanie aside, leaving Tracy to go in alone.

I can't hear him, and I can't imagine what he's telling her. As far as Stephanie knows, Leo and I haven't spoken in a year!

After what seems like for ever, he runs back and joins me behind the bush. "All taken care of," he says, tossing his helmet back on. "Ready to go?"

"Um, aren't you going to tell me what you said to her?"

"All I said was that I called you this morning to wish you a happy birthday and that your mom told me you were home sick. Then I said that your mom said to tell your friends not to call until after school in case you're sleeping."

I consider his story. "You know, you're pretty good at making up stories. You should be a writer."

He smiles mysteriously. "Maybe I already am."

"Meaning?"

"C'mon, it's time for the next stop. You'll see when we get there."

So once again I follow Leo blindly through town, the warm breeze whipping through my hair. The only people out and about are moms with young kids, and the occasional couple holding hands. Leo pulls up in front of the last place I'd expect – the Senior Citizen Community Centre.

Chapter Fifteen

"What are we doing here?"

Without answering me, Leo hops off his scooter, turns it off, and pushes it right through the open doors of the Community Centre. Open mouthed, I don't move until he sticks his head back out and says, "C'mon! It's about to start!"

"*What's* about to start?" But he's already ducked back in. Inside I find the last thing I expected to see — a group of twenty or so white-haired people clapping for Leo, who is stepping up onto a small wooden stage. The steps creak under him and he has to reach up to pull out the microphone from the tall metal stand. My mouth goes dry. What is he *doing*?

Hands visibly shaking, he pulls a piece of paper out of his back pocket and unfolds it. He leans into the mike and says, "I wrote this last year, after I said some not very nice things that hurt a friend of mine."

"Louder!" an old man in the back row yells, twisting a hearing aid in his ear.

Leo quickly moves the mike closer to his face. It bonks him on the mouth and squeaks loudly through the speaker on the wall. "Sorry!" Leo says as the audience cringes.

I sink down into a rickety folding chair, finally noticing the large poster on the wall behind him announcing OPEN MIKE POETRY READING EVERY FRIDAY MORNING. In a voice that gets steadily stronger, Leo recites a few lines about friendship and birthdays and I think it rhymes but I'm too stunned to follow it.

When he's finished the audience claps politely. I realize I've been holding my breath since he started. Leo awkwardly sticks the mike back on the stand, making the audience grimace again as it squeals. He hurries off the stage, grasping his paper tight in his hand. I jump up and we meet in the back of the room as the next poet slowly makes her way up the stairs.

As soon as we get outside I say, "Wow, I can't believe you did that!"

He reddens. "Like in a good way or a bad way?"

"A really good way. You were so brave. That poem was about me, right?"

"What? No, of course not. It was about some other friend who I said something mean about on our birthday." We both laugh.

"But I thought you don't read your poetry in front of people?"

"I don't," he says. "I mean, I haven't before. But that's what today's all about, right?"

"If you say so."

"I'm glad you feel that way because the next stop is all about you!"

"About me?"

Instead of answering, he hands me the folded poem. "You keep this," he says. "As a souvenir of our day."

I'm tempted to read it now since I missed half of it before, but I don't want him to know that. I push the poem deep into my pocket and ask, "How'd you find out about the reading anyway?"

He hops on his scooter and winks. "I have my ways. Now c'mon, let's go eat."

I follow for about ten minutes until we get to the park. Leo pulls up to a vender selling hot dogs and sodas. He's already paid for all of them before I can even pull my helmet off. "Happy birthday," Leo says, clinking his Coke can against mine.

"Happy birthday," I reply, clinking back. A few men and women in business clothes turn to look, and one or two give us second glances, but no one bothers us. Good thing my mom doesn't work in town. She'd freak out if she saw us here.

As I take a bite of my hot dog, I think of Tracy and how against eating meat she is and how she never tells anyone else not to, and how Emma had brought in that cupcake for me and I won't even be there to eat it. They've been really good friends to me this year, and I've been so caught up in my own stuff that I've sort of ignored them. Suddenly I'm not very hungry any more. I pass the hot dog over to Leo, who happily gobbles it up in four bites. He hasn't stopped smiling since his poetry reading. I guess that's what it feels like to do something you're scared of.

After tossing his crumbs to the ducks in the pond, we set off again, this time towards a part of town with a lot of shops. It's getting more crowded on the sidewalks now, so we walk our scooters instead of riding them. We pass shop after shop, including the toy store with its display window full of the cutest stuffed pandas I've ever seen. I press my face against the glass. Leo doubles back and clears his throat impatiently.

"OK, OK," I say, hurrying past the window, "maybe girls do have a thing for stuffed animals after all."

We stop a few stores later, and I look up at the sign. It's the music store where my parents bought me my first drum set when I was eight. To my surprise Leo pushes open the door and bells jangle above his head. I follow him inside. A sign posted on the wall says DRUMMER NEEDED FOR NEW BAND. AUDITION TODAY AT NOON.

Leo grins and points at the sign. I'm not sure what this has to do with us. "I don't get it."

Leo pushes me further into the store. Displays with guitars, basses, drums and violins fill most of the floor space. There's not much room for our scooters, and the clerk behind the counter is watching us warily. Leo takes the scooters and parks them in a corner by a stack of flutes, knocking half of them over. We both scramble to pick them up before we make more of a spectacle of ourselves.

"Leo," I whisper loudly as we're on our knees. "Seriously, what are we doing here?"

He sits up. "You're going to audition to be a drummer in a rock band."

I get to my feet and he follows. I stick my finger in my ear, pretending to clean wax out of it. "I'm sorry, I'm going to do what now?"

He turns me towards a narrow staircase. "They have a soundproof room downstairs. We are going down there together, and you're gonna bang those drums with all you got."

I dig my heels into the carpet. "Oh no, I'm not. You know I've never played in front of anyone."

"I never read my poetry in front of anyone before today, either," he argues, "and I survived."

"But this is different."

"Why?"

"Because it's me!"

Leo rolls his eyes.

A skinny guy with long blond hair pushes the door open. "Dude, they were tough," he says to no one in particular. "They said to send the next guy down."

"You goin'?" asks a deep voice behind us. "'Cause you're blocking the stairs."

"We're going." Leo grabs my arm and practically tosses me down the stairs. At the bottom I find myself facing two guys in their twenties sitting cross-legged on the floor. They're both wearing faded jeans, sandals, and black T-shirts with the words BORN TO ROCK on them. It takes a few seconds for my brain to register that they're identical twins.

They look up at us with identical expressions of expectation and surprise. The one closest to us asks, "You kids lost? The ice-cream shop is next door."

The other chuckles. "Good one, Larry."

"Thanks, Laurence."

Leo clears his throat. "Um, you're both named Larry?"

They shake their heads. The one who spoke first points to his brother. "He's Laurence. Totally different name."

"Our parents had a good sense of humour," Laurence adds.

Leo nods. "They must have."

Larry looks directly at me when he asks Leo, "Doesn't your friend here talk?" I shrink back a bit.

Leo pretends not to have heard him and asks, "Are you the guys looking for a drummer?"

In response, Larry gestures across the room to a drum set. "Hey, you kids gonna interview us for your school paper or something? 'Cause if that's the case, we've got a lotta people to see today."

Leo shakes his head. "You can stop looking because I have your new drummer right here."

The Larrys look around. "Where?"

"Right here," Leo says, pointing to me. I try to duck behind him, but he steps out of the way. I give a half-hearted wave.

The Larrys look amused. "So, you're our new drummer? How long you been playing?"

For some reason I still can't talk.

"Since our second birthday," Leo boasts.

"You remember our second birthday?" I ask, finally finding my voice.

"I remember all our birthdays," he replies.

"She speaks!" Larry says, clapping his hands together.

"Hey, so you guys are twins, too?" Laurence says. "Cool!"

"No, we just have the same birthday," Leo explains.

"So you're twins!" Larry declares. "We gotta let a fellow twin audition."

I open my mouth to explain that we're really not twins, but Leo elbows me in the ribs. "Yup, we're twins all right. Sis here is older by two minutes."

"And I bet she holds it over you every chance she gets," Larry says, nodding knowingly.

"She sure does," Leo agrees, giving Larry a high five.

"Oh, brother," I mutter.

"Come on then, let's hear it," Laurence says, handing me a pair of drumsticks. It feels strange holding someone else's drumsticks. Mine are worn in so my fingers automatically know where to go for perfect balance. I try handing them back, but Leo pushes me towards the drum set. "Remember," he whispers, "no consequences."

I sit down on the stool, feeling foolish. My foot doesn't even reach the pedal for the bass drum. Larry comes over and lowers the stool while I glare at Leo.

I position the drumsticks in my hands, and I admit, it feels good to hold them.

"The traditional grip," Larry says, nodding appreciatively. "Nice. Don't see that much any more."

I KNEW I shouldn't have learned how to play from Dad's old books! I look over the drums. They're much nicer than mine. More cymbals and a row of little drums that my set doesn't have. I move my wrists around, watching the sticks move in circles in the air. Laurence glances at his watch. It's like gymnastics tryouts all over again. But this time instead of my arms, it's the sticks that are waving. I haven't been able to play these last few days and a part of me really wants to let out all my energy, all my frustration, and just bang those drums. But the rest of me just twists the sticks in the air, stalling.

Leo is urging me on with his eyes. Any second, one of the Larrys is going to tell us we're wasting their time. Now or never. *You can do this*, I tell myself. No consequences. Closing my eyes, I picture myself sitting alone in my basement playing. Almost of their own volition, my sticks move towards the snare drum. Inside my head I hear the familiar *one and a two and a three and a four*. My hands move from drum to drum, to high hat, to bass. I keep counting in my head. The sticks are heavier than mine, so it takes a few beats until I feel comfortable controlling them. The sounds the different drums make are deeper and fuller somehow, than mine. These are really excellent drums. My eyes are open now and I'm banging away, like Leo said. I catch his eye and he's grinning, slapping his hand against his leg along to the beat.

A few minutes later Larry comes over and rests his hand on the high hat, just a second before I'm about to hit it. I put the sticks down on my lap.

"You're good, kid," he says. "But we can't take you on account that you ARE a kid. Wouldn't be good for business, you understand."

I nod and hop off the stool, half exhilarated, half glad it's over. My arms are a little shaky as I hand him back the sticks.

"Thanks for coming in, though," Laurence says. "Here, have this." He tosses me what looks like a black ball. It turns out to be a rolled-up black T-shirt like the ones they're wearing. He gives one to Leo, too. We hold them up to our chests. Leo's might fit him in a year or so, but mine looks like it will be a nightgown for years to come.

"Thanks," I tell the twins as they walk us to the stairs. "Thanks for letting me play. It was fun." And it WAS fun. It really was.

"No problem. Come back in ten years. And send down the next guy. Or girl. Or whoever."

We bound up the stairs two at a time and tell

the guy who was waiting there before that he can go down. When we get outside, Leo says, "You were awesome! You were definitely born to rock!"

"And I have the T-shirt to prove it!"

"I know I pushed you into that, I mean, I know I actually had to *push* you, but seriously, you were really good."

"It was fun. But no more pushing. I'm getting bruised!"

"Deal. And to celebrate, let's go to the mall. You can buy anything you want, as long as it's under ten dollars and you have a gift card for it!"

"I don't know about the mall. We'll be the only kids there, people are gonna notice."

"Nah, they'll just think our parents are in another store, or that school got out already. Let's just go for a little while."

"You want to go to the arcade, don't you?"

"Maybe," he admits.

"All right, just for half an hour. I want to make sure I get home long before my dad wakes up."

The Willow Falls mall is on the outskirts of town, near where the old apple grove used to be. By the time we get there my scooter's down to one-quarter power. I hope we'll have enough left to get us home. I wish we had thought to get a lock for the scooters. Leo finds a big bush in the parking lot where we hide them as best as we can. We bring our helmets in with us. Unfortunately the arcade is at the other end from where we enter.

"Try to look casual," Leo whispers.

So we stroll (casually) down the main hallway, sticking close to the storefronts so we don't attract too much attention. Leo lazily swings his helmet. The mall is pretty empty and I start to relax. I've never been to the mall without one of my parents before. If I wasn't so hyper from my audition, I'm sure I'd feel more nervous. I guess I'm just a drum-playing, mall-shopping kinda girl now!

We're about to step on the escalator when a hand grips my shoulder. It's too big by far to be Leo's. I stop in my tracks and turn around. The hand belongs to a mall security guard and he has his other hand on Leo's shoulder. The man looks older than my grandfather. For such an old guy, he has a surprisingly strong grip. Leo's face has drained of its colour. Just like that, the happiness I felt falls to the floor.

"You the Ellerby girl and the Fitzpatrick boy?"

We nod, eyes wide. In a shaky voice, Leo asks, "How do you know our names?"

He relaxes his grip. "Let's take a walk to the security office."

I give Leo a worried look.

"Boy, oh boy," says the officer. "I thought someone was playing a trick on me when I got a missing-kid call with those names. Ellerby and Fitzpatrick, sure! There was a time when that was all you'd hear in this town. But that ain't been for decades."

Leo and I exchange puzzled glances. Maybe this guy is getting senile. He's not making any sense.

He continues, prodding us forward. "But no joke, eh? You two seem pretty real to me."

"What do you mean you got a missing-kid call?" Leo asks. "Who knows we're missing?"

"Everyone, I expect," he says.

The door marked SECURITY looms ahead. I still can't figure this out. Did I forget something when we made this plan? Did my dad forget to cancel my doctor's appointment and Mrs Grayson came over to get me?

Before I can ask the security guard for more information, we hear screaming. "There they are!" Four very anxious parents run up to us. Mom must have left work. Even more surprising,

Kylie is here, too. They all look pretty ragged. Mom's careful make-up is smeared, and Dad is still wearing his blue pyjamas under his jacket. Kylie is pale through her make-up. She glares at me and a blast of anger shoots out of her eyes.

Our parents grab us, hug us, then push us away. "What were you thinking?" my mother yells.

"We've taught you better than this!" Leo's mom says. She tries to yell it, but she can't quite achieve the level of volume my mom can.

Mom's voice is practically shaking with anger. "Imagine how surprised I was, young lady, when your father called me from work to tell me he couldn't find you."

"But I thought Dad was sleeping. . ." I say weakly.

"I was," Dad says, his voice even hoarser than before, "until Mrs Fitzpatrick called to see if Leo was at our house. Imagine my shock when your room was empty. Then imagine all the horrible things that went through my mind about what could have happened to you."

My mouth has gone dry. I don't think he really wants an answer. I also don't think this is a good time to point out that if I had been allowed to own a cell phone, he could have just called me.

"But Mom," Leo says, "how did you know I wasn't in school?"

His mom is still holding him by the arm, as though he might run off again. "You left the sign and streamers for Amanda's locker on your desk. You spent so much time on them last night, cutting out the different letters, trimming the streamers. I didn't want you to be disappointed, so I drove them over to the school. Do I need to tell you the principal doesn't look highly on students forging their parents' signatures?"

Leo looks at his feet and shakes his head.

"Look," Dad says, stroking my hair. "We're glad you're OK, and that the two of you have obviously made up. It was Kylie who suggested we check the gift pile, and sure enough, we found the empty box of gift cards. We figured sooner or later you'd wind up here. I just never would have expected this from you, Amanda." He turns to Leo. "From either of you."

A small crowd has formed, watching the exchange with interest. "Can we go home now?" I ask in a small voice.

"Fine, let's go," Mom snaps. "You'll have a lot of time to think about what you've done while you're sitting alone in your room all night. No birthday cake, no presents, and since your party's already cancelled on account of you being 'sick', we're going to leave it that way."

Leo turns to his parents. "I guess my party's cancelled, too, right?"

His father shakes his head. Leo's face falls, clearly hoping to not have to sit through Hop-along Willie and the Knee-slapping Five again. "We don't want to disappoint your guests. The ones who DIDN'T cut school and give their parents heart attacks. Plus, it's too late to cancel the entertainment. But believe me, the second it's over you're grounded for a long, long time."

Leo and I don't have a chance to speak without being overheard until we're in the parking lot. "Well," he whispers, only moving one side of his mouth. "I did warn you we might get in trouble."

I nod slightly, aware my mother is watching my every move. "Guess I should have let you decorate my locker after all!"

"You're right!" he says, forgetting to keep his voice down. "It's YOUR fault!"

Dad piles both scooters into the trunk of our station wagon, and Kylie and I climb in the back seat. She still hasn't said a word to me. Leo's parents follow us in their car and we both pull up in front of the Schwartzes' house. They make us wheel the scooters up to the front door and apologize for "borrowing" them. It's humiliating. The walk from the Schwartzes' porch to the sidewalk feels a little like walking the plank. This would be a really bad time to have Saturday finally show up.

"Say goodbye to Leo, Amanda," Mom says as we reach the sidewalk and our waiting mothers. "It's going to be a long time till you two spend another birthday together."

"I doubt that," I mumble under my breath. Out loud I say, "Bye, Leo, see you in history class. You know, on Monday."

"Right," he says, stifling a grin. "See you Monday. I've heard a rumour there's gonna be a pop quiz."

Chapter Sixteen

Never in my life have I been so happy to see a balloon. I twirl SpongeBob around the room, dancing like I've just got out of jail. Which in a way I have. Last night was horrible. It was even worse than when Mom thought I had sabotaged her presentation. Even though I apologized like a million times, no one spoke to me. Mom wouldn't even let me talk to Stephanie when she called to find out if I was feeling better. The only good thing to come out of the day is that for the first time, Mom didn't get fired. I guess her boss thought that firing her on the day her daughter goes missing would just be rude. Being grounded gave me time to reflect on everything that's going on, and I can't wait to get to school to talk to Leo.

I leave SpongeBob floating happily and run to

my parents' room. I knock on the door impatiently until Mom opens it, rollers still in her hair. "What is it? Is everything OK?"

I throw my arms around her and hold tight. Laughing, she peels me off of her. "You must be really happy to be turning eleven today!"

"Oh, I am!" I exclaim. "Like you wouldn't believe!"

She steps back a little. "Where'd you get that nightshirt? I don't recognize it."

I look down and am shocked to see the words BORN TO ROCK across my chest. I say the first thing that comes to mind. "I won it at school yesterday. For guessing how many jelly beans were in a fishbowl."

"I see."

"Where's Dad?" I ask, changing the subject.

"He just went downstairs to make some tea. He's not feeling well. I'm sorry but you'll have to take the bus today."

"That's OK!" I say, already halfway down the stairs. I find Dad as he's fishing through the cabinet for a mug. Before he can even turn around I give him a huge hug from behind. He twists to see who it is.

"Well, that's a nice greeting from the birthday

girl," he says, then coughs for a full minute. I don't let go until he's done. Before he can ask why I'm hugging him, I run to the front door and look down the block. I can see Kylie heading back towards the house so I run outside in my bare feet to meet her.

"Whoa!" she says as I plough into her. "What are you DOING? Get off me!"

I hang on tight. "Can't a girl just hug her big sister?"

She stops fighting me. "Are you dying? Am I dying? Did Grandma die?"

I laugh. "No one died."

"Then get off!" She pushes me again, and this time I let go. She runs back into the house, and I follow, whistling happily. Then, suddenly inspired, I run on to the middle of my lawn and do my best back handspring ever. Which is to say that I still didn't do it right, but at least I'm not on my butt on the dewy grass.

I hurry upstairs to get dressed, slipping on the same jeans I wore yesterday, now folded in the drawer, of course. I reach into the pocket to get the poem Leo gave me. It's not there. I check the other pockets. Why would the band's T-shirt have made it across the boundary, but not the poem? I hope Leo has another copy.

I race up the steps of the bus, wishing there was an even faster way to get to school.

"You must really be anxious to get to school," the bus driver says with a smile.

I bob my head up and down. "I am!" I plop in the seat right behind her. Why shout for Stephanie when we can sit right here? The driver hums as she manoeuvers the bus down the tree-lined streets. When I took the bus last month it was a guy driver. This lady is so small her feet barely reach the pedals!

When we get to school I run to my locker, and light up when I see it's fully decorated. And this time there's a folded piece of notebook paper sticking out of it.

"Who's it from?" Stephanie asks, leaning over my shoulder. "A secret admirer?"

I shake my head. "It's from Leo." I wait for her reaction, hoping it was the right decision to say that. But I figure he and I really need to talk, and it's better than hiding from our friends again.

She doesn't even blink. "It's about time you two made up." Guess I don't have to worry about her being jealous.

I reach over and snatch the lollipop from the floor. I place it in her hand.

"What's this for?"

The warning bell rings before I can tell her it's for being a good friend. She jams the lollipop into her pocket and runs down the hall. I take the note into class with me and open it at my desk while Ms Gottlieb writes on the board.

A —
Yesterday was really great. You know, doing all the stuff we'd never have the nerve to do. I hope last night wasn't too horrible for you. I felt so bad that I scared my parents like that. You're so lucky you didn't have your party. Mom glared at me the whole night and all the people from your party came over and it was so hot and crowded. I think most of the kids only wanted to see the hypnotist and Paul the Ball. I'm pretty sure NO ONE wanted to hear the band! Let's just pass notes today, instead of cutting. That didn't work out so good.
— Leo

As I read the note a thought strikes me. As soon as the quiz is graded and handed in, I rip out a piece of notebook paper and write back.

Leo —
I just thought of something. You haven't said
anything about the hypnotist guy. What was
he like? Do you think it's possible that he
could've hypnotized you into thinking every
day was your birthday? And maybe because
it's MY birthday, too, I got sucked in
somehow?
W/B/S.
— A

When Ms Gottlieb's back is turned, I pass the
note to Jimmy and motion for him to pass it to
Claudia next to him, and for her to pass it to Leo.
I hold my breath until Leo gets it. Ms. Gottlieb
has a zero-tolerance note policy and I wouldn't
want that one read out loud.

A few minutes later Jimmy tosses another note
on to my desk.

I don't know. He wasn't that good. All he did
was make Bobby Simon cluck like a chicken.
But maybe we should talk to him, anyway. I
know where to find him. By the way, my
T-shirt from the band is gone. I left it in my
jacket pocket and this morning it was gone. I

*forgot that everything resets itself each
morning.
Bummer!!*
— L

The bell rings before I get a chance to write
back. I wait for him outside class and we walk
down the hall together. He tells me that one of
the school busses goes into town, so we can take
that one to see the hypnotist, and he'll call his
mom at lunch to ask her to pick us up after. Once
that's decided, I tell him I still have my BORN TO
ROCK T-shirt.

"You do?" He wrinkles his brows. "That's
weird. I wonder why yours would stay and mine
wouldn't?"

"I don't know. I wore mine to sleep, and it was
still on me when I woke up."

"That's it!" Leo says, startling me. "Anything
on our bodies stays with us!"

"You're right! The Band-Aids stayed on my
ankles, but when I went to get your poem, it
wasn't in my jeans pocket!"

He stops walking and clutches his books to his
chest. "You know what this means, don't you?"

"That no one should ever dress up as Dorothy

from *The Wizard of Oz* because you'll get blisters?"

"No. Well, *yes*, but that's not it. What it means is that me and you are still growing every day, like normal. But no one else is! So we'll just keep getting older while they stay the same. One day we'll wake up and other people are gonna notice that we don't look the same as the night before."

My jaw slackens. "Oh! You're right! What a horrible thought!"

Leo nods in agreement, his face pale. "This hypnotist better have the answers because I'm gearing up for a growth spurt, I can feel it."

For the rest of the morning this is all I can think about. What if one day I wake up and I look older than *Kylie*??

After school I convince Stephanie (again) that I'm not cut out for the gymnastics team and to try out without me. I decide to experiment with leaving my backpack in my locker to see if it will appear in my house again in the morning. Twenty minutes later Leo and I are standing in front of Willow Falls Pre-owned Vehicles. I don't see anyone nearby. "Your hypnotist works at a *used car lot*?"

Leo nods. "Maybe he hypnotizes people into buying cars."

A middle-aged man in a light blue suit pops out from behind the hood of a white sports car. Leo and I both jump. "Oh, it's you!" Leo says, recovering. "You scared me."

The man wipes his brow with a grey handkerchief. His suit is straining to button across his belly. He doesn't look like he has the power to make anyone buy a pack of gum, let alone cluck like a chicken. "Do I know you?" he asks.

"It's me, Leo!"

I elbow Leo in the ribs.

"Hey, that hurt!"

I give him my most meaningful look.

"Ohhh, right. Got it." Turning back to the man he says, "Er, sorry, I mean it's me, Leo, the kid whose birthday party you're performing at tonight."

The man glances around quickly, maybe looking for Leo's mom. "You're not going to cancel, are you?"

"No, no, nothing like that."

With a sigh of relief, he gives a little theatrical bow. "What can I do for you then? Are you worried I'll embarrass you by making you bark like a dog? Don't worry, I'll save that for some kid you don't like."

Leo and I glance at each other. "Go ahead," I whisper.

"OK," Leo says hesitantly. "This is going to sound really weird..."

"Go on, kid. I've heard 'em all. You want me to hypnotize your mom to give you a later curfew? Bigger allowance?"

Leo looks thoughtful, and I have to jab him again. "OK, OK. No, it's not anything like that. The thing is... my friend Amanda here, we're like, living this day, today, our birthday, over and over."

"Uh-huh," the guy says, smiling at us in that way adults do when they want to humour you into thinking they believe you. Leo doesn't seem to notice.

"And we're wondering," he continues, "if maybe you had something to do with it? Like if you could have hypnotized me into thinking every day was my birthday?"

The guy laughs. "I'm not nearly that good."

Leo's shoulders sag. "Oh."

"Are you sure?" I ask. "Maybe you did it without realizing it?"

He shakes his head. "Believe me, if I could do something like that, I'd hypnotize myself!

Imagine the things you could do if you got a 'do-over' every day!"

"It's not all it's cracked up to be," Leo mutters.

"In all seriousness, kid. Is school stressing you out too much? Family troubles?"

"Come on, Leo." I tug at his sleeve. "Let's go."

"Thanks anyway," Leo says.

The man waves goodbye. "See you tonight!"

"I knew it was a long shot," Leo says as we exit. "What now?"

A green Jaguar parked in front catches my eye. I suddenly remember what Mrs Grayson said when she drove me to the doctor. I tell Leo how my great-great-grandfather was supposedly well-known for some feud in town, like a hundred years ago.

"Really? That's weird. Do you think it had anything to do with what that security guard said at the mall? I've been thinking about that. Why would our last names have meant anything to him? I think we should find that out."

I nod in agreement. "But how? I'm pretty sure my parents don't know anything. They would've mentioned it by now."

"Well, I know some people who might be old enough to remember," he says. "Let's go."

Chapter Seventeen

Five minutes later we're walking into the Senior Citizen Community Centre. I point to a poster advertising the poetry reading. "Maybe they'll let you read your poem again."

"No thanks. I'll read a poem in public again when you play the drums in public."

I think about how good it felt to play the other day. "You never know. I just might surprise you."

"How about those guys?" he asks, pointing to four white-haired men at a card table.

We walk over. For old guys they move pretty quick – tossing cards and plastic coins so fast I can't keep up with whose turn it is. Leo clears his throat. No one looks up. In a loud voice he asks, "Any of you guys a hundred?"

At that, the men all look up and start

guffawing. I groan. Leo's not big on tact. "Please ignore that question," I say, rolling my eyes at Leo. "We were just hoping to ask you about some town history."

One of the guys stops laughing long enough to light his pipe. I glance at the big NO SMOKING sign overhead, but figure he probably doesn't have much time left anyway. Taking a puff, he gestures across the room to a man reading a newspaper on the couch. "Ask ol' Bucky Whitehead. He grew up here, and he's older than dirt."

The others laugh. That wasn't a very nice thing to say. These men could use some lessons on tact, too. I recognize Mr Whitehead from the poetry reading. He had been listening very intently to Leo's poem. When we reach him, I do all the talking.

"We're sorry to bother you, sir, but maybe you can tell us about something that happened in Willow Falls a long time ago?"

He rests his paper on his lap and looks up with kind, milky blue eyes. "Not much happens in Willow Falls," he says with a chuckle.

"That's true," I agree, "but this would have been a really long time ago. Maybe you remember hearing the names Ellerby and Fitzpatrick?"

His expression doesn't change for a minute, and I'm about to thank him for his time when he lets out a low whistle. "Haven't heard those names in the same breath for must be going on eighty years now."

Leo and I share an excited look. We both practically throw ourselves on to the couch and lean forward. "What do you remember about them?" I ask.

He chuckles. "Those folks sure did some crazy things. This was legendary stuff when I was a boy. They'd already patched things up by then, of course."

"Like what kinds of crazy things?" Leo asks.

"Oh, let's see." His eyes close for a few seconds, and I worry he might have fallen asleep. But then he opens them and smiles. "They were neighbours, you know."

We shake our heads.

"Oh, yes. Lived up in Apple Grove. Their farms were Apple Grove, really. Supplied all the town with ripe juicy apples. But they were always in competition with each other. One year Ellerby flooded Fitzpatrick's fields, ruining the harvest for everyone. The next year Fitzpatrick dammed up the river because it ran through his property.

Then Ellerby cut down branches of his own apple trees so no apples would fall on Fitzpatrick's property, things like that. No, they didn't like each other one bit, those two men. And their feud disrupted the workings of the town. People taking sides. Drove everyone crazy."

Leo and I turn to each other, wide-eyed. Could these really be our relatives? "You said they made up at some point, though?" Leo asks.

Mr Whitehead nods. "Strangest thing. No one knows why. One day they were boarding up any window that looked on each other's house, then the next they were the best of friends. Sure, they had a squabble here and there, but nothing lasting more than a few days."

"But what changed things?" I ask, amazed at this story of our long lost relatives.

He shakes his head. "No one knows. Like I said, one day they just patched everything up. Never bothered anyone in town again. I don't think even their own families ever knew what happened. Their secret died with 'em, I expect."

"Is there anything else you can tell us, Mr Whitehead?" Leo asks.

"Call me Bucky," he insists. "Mr Whitehead

was my dad's name. So why do you kids want to know about ancient history anyway?"

"We're kind of related to these people," I say hesitantly. "And you didn't know any of this stuff?"

We shake our heads.

"Young people today," he mutters. "Too much television."

We take that as our cue to go. Leo stands first and reaches out to shake Bucky's hand. "Thank you for your time, Bucky," he says. "We really appreciate it."

He waves us off. "My pleasure. Better than talking about the weather or what's for lunch. That's the usual conversation around here. Come see me anytime."

"We will," Leo promises. I can tell he means it, too.

When we get outside he says, "Wow."

"I know! Wow!"

"Your great-great-grandfather flooded my great-great-grandfather's land!"

"Oh yeah? Well, yours dammed up a river! Whatever that means!"

Soon we're pushing each other and laughing so hard a lady from inside the town's only fancy dress shop asks us to move on down the block.

"Do you think there's some connection?" Leo asks when we've calmed down. "Like between them and what's happening to us?"

"How could there be? The story sounds too crazy to be true. Maybe Bucky made it up."

"Maybe," Leo says, stepping off the kerb without looking. I have to grab him by the collar to avoid him being hit by an SUV. Totally oblivious to his recent brush with death, he says, "But this feels like our only lead. We need to find out more."

"How? If our parents knew anything they'd have told us."

"But they named us after them. That must mean *something*."

"I think they had already named us before they met."

"Hey, I know!" Leo yells, grabbing my arm. "How about we hold a séance and ask our great-great-grandparents what their secret was?"

I roll my eyes and uncurl his fingers from my wrist. "Let's call that Plan B."

"Then what's Plan A?"

"I don't know yet, but I'm pretty sure we can't contact the dead."

"A week ago you'd have said you were sure one day couldn't loop over and over again."

OK, he had a good point there. I glance up at the sun-shaped clock in the town centre. Almost 4:30. Only a few minutes before we have to meet Leo's mom. Leo said she was so excited to hear we're friends again that she almost dropped the phone. It'll be nice to see her when she isn't furious at us. But how many times could we do this over and over again? We NEED to figure it out before I have to pretend one more time not to know a stuffed raccoon lives in the Historical Society.

"That's *it*!" I shout. This time I'm the one grabbing Leo in a death grip. "The Willow Falls Historical Society! If there's any place in town that might know something, it's there."

A honking car makes both of us jump. Leo's mom is waving out the window with a huge grin. "That's a good idea," he says in a low voice as we cross the street towards the car. "Same after-school plan as today?"

As I nod in agreement, his mom jumps out of the car and pulls me into a huge hug. "Amanda! You got so tall! You're sure you're only eleven?"

"Maybe a little older than that," I mutter into her shoulder.

"How'd this reunion happen?" she says,

releasing me and whisking us into her back seat. "Leo didn't give me any details on the phone."

"It's kind of a long story, Mom," Leo says. "Can I tell you tomorrow?"

He winks at me as he says this and I stifle a laugh.

"Sure, keep me in suspense, why don't you," she complains as we head across town towards my house.

"Can I ask you something, Mrs Fitzpatrick?"

She glances back at me in the rear-view mirror. "You know Leo just felt terrible about what happened, don't you, darling?"

"Mom!" Leo complains.

"Oops, sorry, honey. Go on, Amanda, you can ask me anything."

"What do you know about the people Leo and I were named after?"

Without even pausing she says, "Oh, that family feud thing? Didn't we ever tell you about that?"

"Um, NO!" Leo cries out.

"Not much to tell. Way back our two families shared some kind of apple orchard. They used to fight over whether the apples that landed on the Fitzpatricks' property were rightfully his since they came from the Ellerbys' tree."

"But what happened after the feud?" Leo asks.

His mom shrugs. "They made up, I guess. In their wills they left Apple Grove to the town so the town would always have apples."

"But isn't that where the mall is now?" I ask as we pull up to my house. "In Apple Grove?"

She nods. "That's progress for ya."

"But how did they make up?" Leo asks.

"I really don't know, honey. Maybe they just realized a few apples weren't worth all the hassle."

Leo crosses his arms over his chest. He's not convinced and neither am I.

Mrs Fitzpatrick gets out of the car to give me one last hug. "You'll come over first thing in the morning and tell me how you two made up, right?"

"Um, sure. And thanks for driving me home."

She wipes away a tear. Leo rolls his eyes, but I think it's really sweet. I'll never get tired of her being happy to see me. I duck my head into the back and whisper, "Have fun with Hop-along Willie!"

"Have fun with the blisters!"

"See you in history class," I reply. "Don't forget to study!" he calls out.

And when my party ends, after I've comforted Mom about losing her job and shredded my Dorothy costume into the trash can, I *do* study. But instead of history, I use Kylie's science textbook from last year to draw a chart of the periodic table. You never know when it might come in handy.

Chapter Eighteen

I reach over to shut off my alarm, not even remotely surprised any more that it's going off without me setting it. It takes only a few seconds to realize that I left the periodic table in my notebook, which means all the work I put into it last night is gone. Sorry, Bee Boy, I tried. My backpack is waiting for me downstairs, as I suspected it would be even though I had left it in my locker. Still, I give a little jump when I see it. There are some things about this whole day looping over and over that I admit are pretty cool.

I've decided that today I'm going to tell Stephanie about not going to tryouts during lunch rather than waiting till after school. This way Leo and I will have more time to go to the Historical Society. Leo's mom is going to pick us up from school and take us there. So at lunch before everyone begins the usual conversation about my party and Leo's party, I pull her aside and tell her.

"Does this have to do with the marching band?" she demands, the same as she does every time. My usual answer is no, but this time I say, "Maybe. I'm not sure."

"Are you going to try out?" she asks. I can tell by the way she's holding her breath that she really wants me to say no. It wouldn't be very good for our popularity ranking next year.

"No – I mean, at least not today."

"But today's the only day they're holding auditions."

"I guess I'll have to wait till next year," I say, knowing very well I'll get another chance tomorrow. But as I say it, it occurs to me that even if I did try out and I made it, it's not like I'll ever get the chance to actually BE in the band if every day is today. Ugh. We've got to find a way to make this stop.

"I have to go to the bathroom," I tell her.

"Do you want me to come?"

I shake my head. "It's OK. I'll be right back."

I glance over at Leo's table, but he's not there.

We had agreed to meet in the courtyard to go over the plans for later. I hurry out, hoping he hasn't been waiting too long. I purposefully choose not to go down Bee Boy's hall so I don't have to feel bad about forgetting to bring him his project. As I'm rounding the bend past the guidance office, I see Mrs Philips in the doorway talking to Leo. He must be cancelling his appointment for after school. I back quickly out of the way so they don't see me.

"Seriously," he's saying, "I don't need to come after school. Everything's fine."

"Are you certain?" she says. "Your gym teacher said things have got pretty bad with Vinnie."

"It's fine," Leo insists. "I don't care any more what he says to me."

"Perhaps it would be wise not to leave your poetry journal where the boys can see it or they'll keep teasing you."

"Yeah, probably. But that's not even why they're so mean to me. It's just stupid. It's not like I even want to be their friend anyway."

Mrs Philips puts her hand on Leo's shoulder. "OK, Leo. It sounds like you're holding up fine. If you don't let them bother you, it will take their power away."

"OK, thanks."

"I'm here if you want to talk."

Leo nods and hurries away. Unfortunately he hurries right towards me and I don't have any time to scramble backwards.

"Oh," he says when he sees me. "Guess you heard that?"

"Yeah, sorry. I didn't mean to eavesdrop."

Neither of us say anything as we walk towards the courtyard. When we get there, Leo says, "Vinnie and those guys have been teasing me ever since our party last year. That's why I had to go to the guidance counsellor."

"But why are they teasing you? I heard you tell them those things about me. You said that's what they wanted to hear, right?"

"Yeah, but after my mom came to tell me you left the party, I told Vinnie I hadn't meant any of that stuff. That I'd much rather be your friend than his friend."

My eyes widen. "You *did*?"

He nods. "Yeah, and ever since then Vinnie gives me a hard time when he sees me. He had himself a good laugh over my poetry journal. For the past few days I keep trying different things with him. Yesterday I ignored him when he started teasing me. The day before I actually invited him to my party but he didn't come. And today I came up with a really good zinger. But none of them worked. I don't care if he's not my friend any more, but I don't want him to be my enemy."

"I bet he'll come around. Maybe he needs more time."

Leo grits his teeth. "I'll never know if we can't figure out a way to make this day stop."

"I already told Stephanie about not going to tryouts, so we can leave for the Historical Society right after school."

"Sounds good. My mom thinks we're going for a school project."

"Got it."

We part ways and I gear myself up for another smooshed cupcake birthday surprise. I must be a pretty unobservant person not to notice Leo was getting picked on for a whole year. All I had thought about was how I felt; I had never looked at it from his side. We could have made up a whole lot sooner.

After school Mrs Fitzpatrick greets me with the same huge hug as last time, and I happily let her gush over me until Leo leans in and honks the horn impatiently. When she pulls the car up in front of the Historical Society, Leo asks her if she'd mind if we go in alone since it's a school project and all. "I'll be in the dress shop next door. I wouldn't want to cramp your style."

"Your mom talks funny sometimes," I tell Leo as we close the car doors.

"I know. But she's cool."

We walk up to the converted house and I turn the wooden doorknob. The door sticks a little, but I give it a little push and it creaks open. It looks just as it did when we were here on our last school trip. Dusty furniture, old books and ledgers, a bed, and sure enough, a rocking chair with a stuffed raccoon. I peer at it closely. It's pretty gross, actually. Hard to believe I had missed it.

"What do you think it's stuffed *with*?" I whisper to Leo. He shakes his head. "I don't even want to think about it."

"Can I help you folks?" a small, square-shaped old woman asks from behind the information desk. "Something particular you're looking for?"

I can't tear my eyes away from the raccoon, so Leo walks over first. I hear him say, "Wow, that's a big birthmark," and I cringe. We've GOT to have a conversation about tact!

Fortunately she laughs. "Some people think it looks like a duck."

At that, I slowly turn and join Leo. The woman turns towards me and the light catches the left side of her face. I gasp. I've seen that duck before.

"Aren't you my . . . my bus driver?"

She smiles broadly. "I get around."

"But if you're here, then who's driving the bus right now?"

"I only drive in the morning," she explains.

"Oh."

"Can we focus here?" Leo asks.

"Sorry. We're looking for something that maybe you can help us with?"

She opens her arms wide. "Got a lotta stuff here, and no one knows the history of Willow Falls better than me. Ask away."

"We need to find out more about the feud between the Ellerbys and the Fitzpatricks."

She looks amused. "Now that really IS going far back." She points to a rolltop desk on the other side of the room. "That there was old man Fitzpatrick's desk. Did all his business there."

"Really?" Leo says. "That was my great-great-grandfather's desk?"

"And that," she points to an old-fashioned record player, "is Mrs Ellerby's prized possession, her phonograph."

"My great-great-grandmother liked music!" I say excitedly, thinking of my drum set.

"Come look at this," the woman says, leading us over to the far wall. The whole wall is covered in old maps and blueprints of the town. She points to one of the maps. "This is a survey of the town a little over a hundred years ago. Each little box indicates someone's property." We lean in to see where her finger's pointing. Two boxes right next to each other are clearly marked ELLERBY and FITZPATRICK in tiny block letters. Little drawings of apple trees dot the area around the squares.

"What about their feud?" Leo asked. "Do you know anything about it?"

"The whole town knew about it," she says. "Turned Willow Falls upside down, it did. Rumour was the townsfolk got together to do something about it."

"They *did?*" We hadn't heard that part of the story before! "What did they do?"

The woman leans in closer. So close I can see the duck wiggle when she talks. It's a little distracting. "Rumour has it that they sought the help of an old woman who had special, shall we say, *gifts*, to help fix the situation."

"What kinds of *gifts*?" Leo and I ask together.

The old woman looks left and right before answering, and even though we're alone in the place, she lowers her voice. "Rumour has it on Harvest Day, the men were warned if they didn't solve their differences, there would be consequences."

"What kind of consequences?" I whisper, not sure why we're whispering.

She shrugs, and in her regular voice says, "Whatever it was, it worked. Not right away, not until a year later in fact, but it worked. They became friends seemingly overnight and stayed that way for the rest of their days, except for the occasional squabble that all friends have."

"And they never told anyone what happened to make them stop fighting?"

"Oh, they told someone," she says, flicking a piece of dust off the raccoon's head.

"Who?" we both ask. "Who did they tell?"

She opens her mouth to answer, when the door bangs open and a Girl Scout troop pours in. "Don't touch anything, girls, I'll be right with you. Now where was I?"

"You were about to tell us who knows about the fight?" Leo says impatiently.

"Right. The only person they told was— hey, put that down!" She hurries over to a Girl Scout and pries an antique hairbrush from her hands. Leo and I hurry after her.

"Please Mrs . . . Miss . . ."

"You can call me Angelina."

"Angelina, please," Leo pleads. "Just tell us who knows about the fight." He stands right in front of her so she can't see the Girl Scout with the dripping green ice-cream cone.

"The only person they told was Alexander Smithy, the founder of Willow Falls. He was the kind of man you could confide in. Alexander Smithy never told a soul, although many tried to get it out of him. That man didn't talk much at all, confided everything to his journal instead."

"Is his journal here?" Leo asks, waving his hand at the shelves full of dusty books. "Can we see it?"

I kick him in the shin. "How can you ask that? After a week of taking the same pop quiz, you know exactly what happened to that journal. It was stolen!"

"That's right," Angelina says, nodding.

Leo glares at me and rubs his shin. Then he turns to her and asks, "Do you know who stole it?"

She nods.

"Who was it?" I ask breathlessly.

"Me."

For a minute, we all just look at one another.

"Huh? *You* stole it?" Leo says, recovering first. "But why?"

"I collect such things," Angelina replies, ducking around Leo to keep an eye on the Scouts.

"Do you still have it?" I ask.

She shakes her head. "Lost it years ago in a fire."

Leo and I hang our heads in defeat.

"But it wouldn't matter anyway," she continues. "There was plenty in there about the feud, but nothing after. Unless Ellerby and Fitzpatrick kept journals themselves, the trail is cold. And the only things I've ever seen from those two are business ledgers. Why does this matter to you anyway? It's ancient history."

"We don't really know," I admit. "It's just . . . we're going through a weird thing and then we learned about this feud, and the two of us had been in a fight, and well. . ." I drift off, not knowing how to explain the connection we feel to our great-great-grandparents. It's more than just our names, but how could I explain it?

"Thanks anyway," Leo says glumly. "We better go, my mom's waiting."

"See you on the bus tomorrow, Angelina," I say as we walk to the front door.

"See you then, honey." She waves as she closes the door behind us.

It's not until I'm in bed later that it hits me. Angelina didn't correct me when I said I'd see her on the bus. She didn't say, "No you won't, because tomorrow's Saturday." This keeps me awake for hours.

Chapter Nineteen

As soon as I turn off the alarm that I knew
would ring, I reach into the pocket of the
sweatpants I had worn to bed. Yup! The
periodic table is still there, right where I tucked
it last night. I feel a surge of pride that I was
able to make it stay overnight. I transfer the
folded notebook paper into my jeans, and begin
the all-too-familiar process of my birthday
morning. I freely admit that if Leo wasn't
experiencing this with me, I would completely
lose my mind.

I'm in such a rush to talk to Angelina that I
bound up the bus steps before Kylie. But Angelina
isn't driving! Instead, the young guy I remember
from last month is behind the wheel.

"Move," Kylie orders from behind me.

I don't budge. "Where's Angelina?" I ask him, my voice quivering.

"Who?"

"Our usual bus driver?"

"*He's* our usual bus driver," a kid yells from the middle of the bus. "Are you gonna sit down? You're gonna make us late!"

"C'mon, Amanda, move!" Kylie pushes me forward and I almost fall into the seat behind the driver. I stare at the back of his head the whole ride, wondering what this means. How could she not be here? Why do the other kids think this is our regular guy? I scoot over when Stephanie gets on, and tune out her gymnastics tryouts chatter.

I practically tackle Leo when I see him in the hall. Stephanie and Ruby look on in surprise, but I don't stop. "It's her!" I shout. "It's Angelina!"

"*What's* Angelina?"

"She wasn't my bus driver this morning!"

He clutches my arm. "What? Are you serious?"

Stephanie puts her hands on her hips. "You guys don't talk for a year, and when you do, you don't make any sense!"

I keep talking. "It was some young guy. No one even knew who Angelina *was!*"

Leo shakes his head in amazement. "And it's not like she's easy to forget."

"I know! So what does this mean?"

"It means we have to go back to the Historical Society today. Same plan as before."

"OK, got it."

A crowd has started to form. Leo hurries into the classroom while I face a very confused Stephanie.

"What was that all about?" she asks.

I bend down, scoop up the green-apple lollipop, and present it to her. "I'll tell you tomorrow, OK?"

"This is huge! You want me to wait till tomorrow?"

"It's my birthday," I remind her. "Shouldn't you have to do what I say?"

"Fine!" she says, turning on her heel. "But I'm calling you first thing tomorrow morning!"

"No problem," I say, smiling to myself. *No problem at all.*

• • • • • • • • • • •

I'm standing at a safe distance when Bee Boy bursts through the door, right on schedule. Before he can say a word, I shove my periodic table into his hand. "What ... what's this?" he asks between sniffles. "Who're you?"

"You don't know me, but I have a feeling you might need that. It's a drawing of the periodic table. I actually learned a lot of stuff while making it. Did you know that helium is only found on the sun and lead comes from asteroids?"

He unfolds the paper and looks up in surprise. "How did you know I needed this?"

"Call it a hunch," I say.

He examines my work, a pleased expression on his face. "Um, not to be ungrateful or anything, but did you have to use a purple pen? It's a little, um, girly."

Mr Collins opens the door before I can defend my use of colour. I quickly turn to a nearby locker, and twist the lock like it's my own.

"Have you collected yourself?" he asks.

"I ... I found it!" the boy replies, holding up the paper. He hurries back into his class with a grateful nod in my direction. I am flooded with a sense of accomplishment. I did it! But as good as it feels to have been able to help this kid, I doubt this is the reason Leo and I are in this situation. I look at my watch. Three more hours until we get some REAL answers.

· · · · · · · · · · ·

As soon as Mrs Fitzpatrick is safely inside the dress shop, we run up to the door of the Historical Society. I try to turn the knob, but it won't budge. We both lean our shoulders against it, but nothing happens. "Look!" Leo is pointing to a sign on the door that says CLOSED FRIDAYS.

"But that's not possible!" I cry.

"You're right," Leo says, leaning back against the locked door. "There's definitely something going on here."

For the first time since I knew I wasn't alone in this, a feeling of dread and hopelessness comes over me. It almost knocks me over.

"Are you OK?" Leo says, holding on to my arm. "You look like you're going to faint or something."

I slide down on to the sidewalk, and Leo joins me, our backs against the door. "It's just, I don't know. I feel like she was our last hope."

"I know what you mean."

"And what if she was lying? Maybe that

journal didn't really burn in a fire, and she just wants to keep it from us?"

Leo doesn't answer. Then he jumps up and says, "C'mon."

"Where are we going?" I stand up and hurry after him. He ducks around the side of the old house and into the alley separating it from the dress shop next door. "Leo, wait. What are you doing?"

He keeps going. "We're going to get that journal."

"How? It's closed!"

"Like this," he says, pointing to a window in the back of the house. I glance around us, but no one is nearby. Trees and bushes make things pretty private. Still, there's a tiny parking lot back here, and at any minute someone could pull in. Leo reaches up and pushes up on the window. I had totally expected it to be locked, but it slides up smoothly. "Ready?" He laces his hands together and bends down for me to step on his hands.

"Me? I have to go in first?"

He looks up at me. "Would you rather give me the boost?"

I shake my head. I'm not that strong. With one

last glance around me, I put my hands on his shoulders for balance, and step up. He practically catapults me through the window. It's a good thing there wasn't any furniture on the other side or I definitely would have broken it. As it was, the floor could have been a little softer. I'm gonna have bruises for sure. I brush myself off and lean out the window. Leo is jumping and trying to grab on to the ledge. His hands keep slipping off. I watch his efforts for a few minutes, then call down, "Um, Leo? How about I go open the front door and let you in?"

"Oh, good idea!"

A minute later we start searching the place. I open all the drawers – nightstands, desks, file cabinets. Leo checks the bookshelves and the back room. He even opens the mini-fridge but only finds a half-eaten salami sandwich. He comes back out, his hair a mess from sticking his head under the rugs. I'm in the process of checking the drawers of his great-great-grandfather's desk.

"Nothing, huh?" he asks, joining me at the desk.

I shake my head. "It's empty." But when I go to close the bottom drawer, it doesn't line up evenly with the rest. I push on it with all my strength, but it still doesn't close all the way. This isn't good. Angelina's bound to notice. I wiggle it around, thinking maybe it's caught on something. Hey, maybe it's CAUGHT ON SOMETHING.

"I'm gonna try taking it all the way out instead," I tell Leo excitedly. "I think something's jammed back there!" I pull it as far as it will go, but it won't come all the way out.

"I have an idea," Leo says. I step away. Leo pulls on the drawer above mine and it slides out easily. Now we can easily reach behind the bottom one!

"You can do the honours," Leo says.

I take a deep breath and stick my hand down there. At first all I feel is a thick layer of dust. Then my fingers land on something smooth. I feel around until I find edges that I can grab.

"What is it? What is it?" Leo is bouncing around like a little kid.

I brush off the dust and find myself holding a small black notepad.

"Is it the founder's journal?" he shouts, then covers his mouth with his hands.

Able to read the words on the cover now, I slowly shake my head. "Even better, it's your great-great-grandfather's journal!"

Chapter Twenty

He gasps and reaches for it. I place it in his hands. "It must have been stuck back there all this time. I bet you jarred it loose when you opened the drawers."

I sit next to him as he rubs his fingers over the embossed letters. They're very faded, but the words PROPERTY OF LEONARD FITZPATRICK are still legible.

Suddenly there's a banging on the front door. We jump up so fast I instantly get dizzy. The Girl Scouts have arrived for their tour. Guess they didn't know the place was closed on Fridays, either! "Duck," Leo says, pulling me down behind the desk. "I don't think they saw us."

We stay crouched while the knocking continues. Then the phone rings. The answering machine clicks on and we hear, "Thank you for calling the Willow Falls Historical Society. We are closed every Friday until further notice. Please try us again at another date." The Girl Scout troop leader leaves a not very nice message about how hard it is to coordinate such visits.

The scouts finally leave. We get up and move over to the couch, which is well hidden from the front door. "Here goes," Leo says, opening the small book. The ink is faded to a dull blue. I lean over and he moves the notebook between us. The first few pages are filled with rows of numbers. Then there's a long list of items to get at the shop – tools, wood, milk. Leo flips through the rest until he finds a few pages filled with tiny block letters. He finds the beginning and reads out loud: *"I do not scare easily. I did not act when the strange woman darkened my door with her threats of consequences if Rex Ellerby and I did not end our feud. He and I have never seen eye to eye and I did not imagine we ever would. This is not the place to list my grievances against the man. Suffice to say they are long and varied. It was Harvest Day and I had bigger things on my mind. I have started to record these words many times, only to have them disappear the next day. I have learned to keep them on my person. It is only that way they survive."*

I gasp when Leo reads that part. "That's like us! How we have to keep things on us when we sleep or else we lose them!"

"Do you really think that's what he means?"

"I don't know, keep reading!"

He turns back to the book. *"For endless days now, I have been harvesting my apples. Each time Harvest Day ends, it starts again."*

"I knew it!" I shout, not caring who hears me. "I knew it!"

Leo keeps reading, unable to keep the excitement out of his voice. *"It's always the same. Josephine fixes my eggs, the buggies arrive with the baskets, the men line up in the fields. Why does no one else realize this is happening? It is enough to drive a man mad. And of all people, it seems Ellerby is involved in this thing, too! It took five days until we understood what happened to us. It was that strange old woman. She did this to us. Some kind of enchantment. We searched high and low. She has disappeared. Our mutual situation has forced us to mend our fences. We spent the day helping the townsfolk undo what our ridiculous feud did to the town. We undammed the river so others' land will no longer suffer, told the local businesses we would no longer boycott their goods if they took apples from the other. One hour ago we shook hands like gentlemen and raised our glasses to a successful harvest. Josephine and Amanda were witnesses to it. Almost knocked 'em over, it did."*

A new section starts on the next page. *"It happened! It is now the day AFTER Harvest Day. Ellerby and I ran from our houses and embraced by the river. We jumped around like children while our wives and the townsfolk stared in amazement. We have agreed never to speak of this to anyone."*

Leo flips the rest of the pages, but they're blank. He lets the book fall closed on the floor. When he looks up, his eyes are bright. "Now we know why this happened to us!"

"We do?"

"Don't you see? They ignored the old woman's warning and kept fighting, then after the one-year-mark passed, they got stuck in the loop. You and me got into a fight last year on our birthday, so *this* year on our birthday the enchantment or whatever it was, kicked in. I guess 'cause we're related to them?"

I jump up, almost hitting my head on a low shelf. "You're right!" Relief floods through me. The pieces of the puzzle are finally coming together.

"OK, so somehow we're reliving the same thing our great-great-grandfathers did," Leo says, starting to pace. "We know they eventually broke out of the loop. What we don't know is *how*."

"Yes, we do." I pick up the small book and wave it in the air. "Leonard told us."

"What do you mean?"

"He wrote about how he and Rex made up, and then how they helped the townspeople and made everyone happy, right? So that's what we have to do!"

"But we made up a week ago," he points out, "and it's still happening. And I tried to fix things with Vinnie, but nothing changed. You tried to help your mother and she still got fired."

"That's true," I admit, my hope deflating.

"Then again . . . you did help that kid with his science project, and your sister with hers, and those worked out, right?"

I nod. "Yeah. Maybe some things you can change, and some you can't."

"So tomorrow we help everyone we come across, whether we think we can make a difference or not."

"Deal." We shake on it. "I have a really good

feeling about this."

"Me too," he says.

Then the two of us look at each other, let out a whoop, and bounce around just like old Rex and Leonard did. We're so busy high-fiving and whooping and jumping on the couches, we don't hear the knock on the door until it turns into more of a pounding. We were supposed to meet Leo's mom at the dress shop, but we must have lost track of time. We hurry over to the door and unlock it. She points to the sign.

"How come it says closed on Fridays if you're inside? And why was the door locked?"

I have to catch my breath from all the jumping before coming up with an answer. "The lady who worked here? She had to um, step out, so she locked the door behind us so no one could come in."

Leo nods in agreement.

"Oh," his mom says. "Well, did you find what you were looking for?"

"And more!" replies Leo. "I just need to put a book back." While he re-hides the journal, I keep Mrs Fitzpatrick occupied by showing her the stuffed raccoon, which grosses her out as much as it does me.

As we walk to the car Mrs Fitzpatrick's eyes

fill with tears. She looks from Leo to me and back again. Leo's eyes narrow. "Mom," he warns, "you're not going to cry because Amanda and I are friends again, are you?"

"I might," she says, laying her hand on her chest. "It's just so wonderful. Does your mother know yet, Amanda?"

It honestly takes me a few seconds to remember if, in this version of our birthday, my mother knows or not. I shake my head. "Not yet."

"She will when I bring you home!" she says, linking her arm in mine.

"She won't be there. Big day at work."

"Oh." She frowns. "Well, we'll all get together tomorrow and talk about old times."

"Tomorrow, definitely!" I say as sincerely as I can muster. I have to kick Leo to keep him from laughing.

When we get to the car Leo starts to open the front door. "In the back, kiddo."

Leo groans and mutters, "It's up to us to save the world from repeating the same day over and over, but we're still not allowed to sit in the front seat."

"Is that what we're doing?" I whisper as he slides in next to me. "Saving the world or saving ourselves?"

"Maybe it's the same thing," he whispers back.

I think about that while Mrs Fitzpatrick rambles on and on about how we need to celebrate the renewal of our friendship. Could we actually be saving the world? I never thought turning eleven would bring such responsibility. I would have stayed ten!

Chapter Twenty-One

I turn off my alarm with a new sense of purpose. Today I must pay close attention to what's going on around me. I don't want to miss a single opportunity to help anyone. I grab an extra notebook from my desk and title the first page: THINGS I DID TODAY THAT HELPED PEOPLE. By first period, this is what my list looks like:

1. Untwisted one of SpongeBob's streamer arms. He looked uncomfortable. I'm sure he would have thanked me if he wasn't, you know, a balloon.

2. Brought Dad a goody bag full of sick-person stuff — tissues, lozenges, bags of

tea, a Peanuts anthology (he loves Charlie Brown and I heard laughing when you're sick helps you get better), and pink eye-shades. He was very grateful and said I was an excellent daughter.

3. Exchanged posters between Mom and Kylie. Mom hugged me, and Kylie grunted. I'm pretty sure I heard a "thank you" embedded in the grunt. I told Mom that I hope her presentation goes well, but that she's a great person and her job is not a measure of her worth. (I came up with that after looking online last night for "things to say when someone you love gets fired".)

4. When Ruby climbs on the bus I offer to help her with her large duffel. She does not accept my help.

5. When Stephanie gets on the bus I offer to help her, too, and she says, "sure," and then gives me a birthday hug.

6. When I get to my locker I pick up the lollipop and ask everyone in the vicinity if it is theirs. Vinnie Prinz says it's his! I give it to him and he says, "Sucka!" so I guess it really wasn't his after all.

7. When Suzanne Griggs announces she doesn't have a pen for the test, both Leo and I jump up to give her one instead of letting Ms. Gottlieb do it, which is what has happened every other time.

I'm about to stick the notebook back in my bag and start the quiz when Ms Gottlieb appears at my side. She holds out her hand. "The rest of the class removed their belongings from their desk for the pop quiz when I asked. Yet still you scribble. What are you writing so intently, Miss Ellerby? Not planning on cheating on the quiz, are you?"

"No, of course not," I reply shakily. I've never been accused of cheating before.

"I'll be watching you," she says. She walks away slowly, her eyes never leaving mine.

"Yikes," Leo mouths from across the room. I sink into my chair. Just to be on the safe side, I

219

get a few answers wrong.

Bee Boy is as happy today as yesterday when I give him the periodic table. Happier even, because this time I drew it in black pen. At lunch I make sure to do a better job of cutting the cupcake so it doesn't crumble. A small thing, I know, but I'm not taking any chances. After the last bell rings I force myself to go to the gym and change back into my gym clothes. I know that if I made the team, it would be helping out Stephanie, so I have to do this for her. When I see Ruby in the locker room and she asks me in that snide way of hers if I'm excited about tryouts, I answer honestly that I'm not likely to make it, but that I'm sure she will. Instead of telling me about other girls freezing up like she did in the past, this time she actually gives me a small smile.

As I'm standing up there with Stephanie cheering me on, I suddenly understand something. I *can* do a back handspring. And not only because I've practised over the past few days. I probably could have done it the first time. I was just scared. But it would take a lot more to scare me now, after everything I've been through. So I swing my arms a few times to get momentum, and then fly backwards, my hands landing perfectly behind me. Well, not perfectly, exactly, but at least they land and I don't fall. Stephanie and some of the other girls clap for me, and I return to the bench with a spring in my step.

"That was amazing!" Stephanie squeals, grabbing my arm. "I've never seen you do that before!"

"Oh, I've been doing that for years," I reply, laughing. Instead of running out to wait for her mom to pick us up, I sit with the other girls. Coach Lyons consults her clipboard for a few minutes while we grasp hands. Mena, Heather, Jess and the other girls who are already on the team stand with her while she reads off the list of the girls who made it. Ruby's name is called first, then two other girls who I don't know very well, then the transfer student Jana Morling, then Stephanie, and then last of all, me! I made it! I'm kind of stunned. I used to love gymnastics. Maybe this will be a good thing? Stephanie's really happy and on the way home her mom takes us all for ice cream.

When I get home I tiptoe in so I don't wake Dad on the couch. He's wearing the pink eyeshades I gave him this morning. I carefully tuck his blanket around him. Instead of hiding up in my room, I finish setting up the basement for the party. If all goes according to plan, this will be the last time I have to do this.

Instead of only eight kids, this time thirteen show up! All the other kids who made the gymnastics team are here! They came with Stephanie. Everyone's having a good time dancing (I replaced Dad's CD selection) when the phone rings. It's too early for Mom to get her bad news, so I can't imagine who it could be.

"It's Leo!" Mom says excitedly, shoving the phone at me. She motions for my dad to turn off the CD player. Everyone crowds around. Leo and I had kept our distance all day so as not to complicate things. Now I'm going to have to pretend this is our first conversation in a year.

"Um, hello?" I say.

"I'm not on speaker, am I?" Leo says quickly.

"No, but everyone's hanging on to my every word," I warn. My friends grin and move even closer. I cup my hand over the phone. "So, um, what's up?"

"I think we better have our parties together," he says. "The journal says they celebrated the harvest together. Maybe we have to do that, too, or it won't work!"

Loudly, I reply, "You say you're really sorry for everything you said? You have a big present for me and want me to bring everyone over?" The crowd squeals in delight.

On the other end of the phone Leo groans. "Yeah, yeah, laugh it up. Just get everyone over here."

"OK, I'll try. Happy birthday to you, too!"

"Oh, right, happy birthday." He hangs up and I hand the phone back to Mom who looks like she's going to burst.

Everyone's watching me expectantly. "Um, how would you all like to see a really great band?"

It's unanimous. Everyone wants to go. I suggest to Mom that she invite Mrs Grayson, who is surprised but seems excited to come. Between the three cars we're able to fit everyone.

On the way there Stephanie keeps pestering me. "So exactly what did he say? Are you guys friends now?" I give her my standard reply, "I'll tell you tomorrow." Then I realize if this works, I'll actually have to make good on that promise!

"Nice shoes," Leo says as soon as I step out of the car.

"You haven't spoken to me in a year, and that's

223

the first thing you say?"

He looks around at the crowd surrounding us. "Um, sorry, I mean, hey, great costume!"

I look past him and can't stifle my gasp. Tiki torches line the path from the driveway to the whole backyard, where a huge tent has been set up, complete with hanging strobe lights. I even spot a cotton-candy machine! I grab Leo by the sleeve and tell the group, "Go have fun, Leo and I have a few things to talk about in private." I drag him to the far side of the yard.

"A *tent*? Cotton *candy*? I think you left out a few details about your party. You could have just told me. I'd have found out anyway."

Before he can answer, a boy holding cotton candy in one hand and a snow cone in the other calls out, "Great party!"

I grit my teeth. Leo gives a half-hearted wave in return and says, "I figured if tomorrow never came, no one would tell you about it."

I watch as some huge guy in an orange-and-black football uniform – who could only be Paul the Ball – teaches a group of adoring boys how to properly hold a football. I know it shouldn't matter after everything we've been through, but it does. To think that this is how he was celebrating his birthday without me really hurts.

"Look," he says quietly, "I told you I didn't ask for this. It only made me feel worse, not better, that you weren't here."

I kick at the grass with my red shoe. I wish I'd gone upstairs to change before coming over.

Leo steps a little closer. "You're here now, right? So this is OUR party, not my party."

At that moment Bobby Simon walks by. "Cluck, cluck!" he says with a wave.

I can't help but smile. "Guess I missed the hypnotist?"

Leo nods. "Yup, poor Bobby. He doesn't have a clue. The hypnotist said it will wear off by tomorrow."

I watch Bobby greet Mena, Heather and Jess with clucks. They laugh at him. He slinks away, confused. "If we can't make tomorrow come, he'll be clucking for the rest of his life!"

"There you are," my mom says, reaching out her arms and giving Leo a big hug. "I've missed you, you little rascal!"

Leo grins and lets my mom ruffle his hair and pinch his cheeks. My mom's not usually the cheek-pinching type. Dad comes up from behind and slaps Leo on the back. He might have been a little overenthusiastic because he almost knocks Leo over. Dad starts to apologize but ends up in one of his sneezing fits. Across the yard the band is starting up. Raising his voice over the twang of the electric banjo, Leo says, "Run, save yourselves. Trust me, you don't want to hear this."

"Nonsense," my dad says, swinging my mom around to the dance floor. "This is knee-slappin' music!" Mom gig- gles and lets herself be twirled around.

Leo leans in closer and shouts, "I guess she didn't get fired yet?"

I shake my head and shout, "I took her cell phone out of her purse before we came!"

Leo nods appreciatively. "Nice!"

"Let's go inside," I shout.

We make our way through the crowd of laughing kids – many holding their hands over their ears – and stumble into the kitchen. Piles of plastic cups line the countertop, along with soda and juices of every kind. Leo pours us each a cup of lemonade and says, "A hundred years ago, our great-great-grandfathers made a toast to their friendship, so I thought we should, too."

He raises his cup into the air, but I lower mine. "Are we just doing this because they did it?"

"What do you mean?"

"Having our party together, and this toast. Are we doing it to break the enchantment, or because we want to?"

He lowers his own cup. "Well, if all this wasn't happening to us, wouldn't you still want to have our parties together?"

"Yes," I say without hesitation. "And if I had to be stuck in time with anyone, I'm glad it's you."

"Me too." He raises his cup again and I tap mine to it. We both drink and then grab our throats. He chokes out the words, "Real lemons, no sugar."

Stephanie walks in, arm in arm with Mena. "Hey, Leo!" she says. "Great party! Really bad band!" Mena just looks bored. But that's how she usually looks.

"Nice ears," Leo says, pointing at Stephanie's elf ears. Stephanie unlinks her arm and reaches up. When she feels them, her face reddens and she tugs them off.

"So, Amanda," Mena says, digging through a bowl of chips. "You'll have to work on that back handspring over the summer if you want to be ready to compete."

"Compete?" Leo asks, turning to me.

"Oh, yeah. I made the gymnastics team!" I say with more excitement than I feel. I hadn't thought at all about the competing part.

"You *did*?" Leo couldn't be more shocked. "Wow, you've been busy today."

"C'mon, Steph," Mena says, "let's go find the bathroom." They link their arms together again, and Steph waves as Mena pulls her down the hall.

"I only tried out because I thought it would help Stephanie, you know, to have me with her on the team."

"But I thought you didn't want to do it."

"I just want this birthday to end. I wasn't really thinking about the consequences. It doesn't really matter. I'm the worst person on the team, I'll probably never have to compete."

Kids are starting to make their way inside, away from the band. Jimmy Dawson calls out, "Hey, Dorothy, how's Oz these days?" but he says it in a nice way.

Before we're completely surrounded, Leo whispers, "If we did everything right today, then you'll have the whole summer to practise. And if we didn't, you'll just have to try out again tomorrow."

"We did," I whisper confidently. "I know we did. What more could we have done?"

Leo's mom sticks her head in the room. "Amanda! You're wanted on the dance floor!"

I put any doubts out of my mind as I let Mrs Fitzpatrick drag me on to the dance floor where I finally get to kick off my shoes. The band is playing some kind of jig that's totally impossible to dance to, but I'm having fun. I finally feel right where I'm supposed to be – celebrating my birthday with Leo and all our friends and families. For a split second I think I catch sight of Angelina by the snow cone machine. Does she know about the break-in? Is she going to tell our parents? But when I look closer, it's just a crowd of kids jostling to scoop out cups of purple ice. I shake my head to clear it of the image of a waddling duck. After all, Leo put the journal back behind the drawer, and we closed the back window. At least I'm pretty sure we closed the back window.

If we forgot, we'll just go tomorrow and apologize. Maybe even volunteer for a couple of hours answering visitors' questions about Willow Falls's history. Somehow Angelina is involved in all this. And someday I'd like to know how. But for now it's enough that it's over. Tomorrow I'm going to sleep for a long, long time. And then I'm going to open my presents.

Chapter Twenty-Two

Nothing in the whole entire world sounds worse than the beep beep beep of my alarm clock. When I hear it this morning I lie still at first, in utter disbelief. Then I calmly get out of bed, unplug the alarm clock, and throw it out the window with all my might. It tangles in the tree branches then falls with a satisfying crash on to the dirt below. I'm about to kick the SpongeBob balloon, but before my foot strikes his yellow sponge belly, I make myself stop. It's not his fault he's still here.

Like a zombie, I get dressed and scribble the periodic table that I hadn't made last night because I didn't think I'd need it. Before Kylie gets back from her run I duck into her room to use the phone she got installed last month for her thirteenth birthday.

231

Leo's dad answers on the first ring. Instead of a simple hello, he says, "Top of the morning to you," when he picks up.

"Um, this is Amanda, can I speak to Leo?"

"Amanda!" he thunders happily. "So wonderful to hear your voice! Happy birthday!"

"It's not that happy," I mutter.

"Leo's going to be thrilled to hear from you," he continues. "He's been moping around all morning. He feels terrible about what happened last year, you know."

"I know."

"Let me put him on. I hope we'll see you tonight?"

I sigh. "Pretty sure you will."

Leo gets on the phone. His dad must still be standing there because Leo says, "Amanda! So great to hear from you. I'm so sorry about our fight. I was a total jerk. Let's make up. What's that? You forgive me? You're the best! I'll meet you when your bus pulls into school and we'll talk."

When he finally pauses to take a breath, I ask, "Leo, what did we do wrong?"

"I don't know," he replies, "but we're going to find out." His voice muffles a bit and I figure he's got his hand over the mouthpiece. "Keep doing what the journal said. Help whoever you can."

"What are you doing?" Kylie demands, walking in on me.

"Gotta go," I tell Leo. "See you at the bus stop."

"I'm sorry for using your phone," I tell her, not up for a fight right now. "I needed to call Leo."

"Leo?" she asks, clearly caught off guard. "Why? Shouldn't he be the one to call you after all this time?"

I want to point out that she's the one who's planning on asking a boy out today, but that wouldn't go over very well. I answer honestly. "This is a really hard day for me. I woke up this morning and really needed to talk to him."

Grabbing her clean clothes from her drawers, she says, "Why is this such a hard day for you? It's only your eleventh birthday. Try turning thirteen, that's MUCH harder."

"That's just it!" I shout, finally cracking. "It's NOT only my eleventh birthday. It's my ELEVENTH eleventh birthday!"

"Huh?"

I throw up my hands in despair. "I'm never going to HAVE a thirteenth birthday! I'm never going to have a SATURDAY again!"

She stares at me, her clothes dangling at her sides. "Uh, maybe you should talk to Mom and

Dad about whatever you're, uh, going through. I need to get in the shower."

I grab the pink T-shirt from her hand. "Please, PLEASE, wear something else! I can't see you in this one more time!"

She snatches it back from me. "I haven't worn this shirt for three weeks! Now get out of my room! We have to take the bus today and you're going to make us miss it!" She points to the door and I storm through it. She goes into the bathroom and slams the door. I'm at a loss for what to do. Might as well still help who I can, like Leo said. I gather the stuff for Dad's get-well bag, and present it to him in the kitchen. He wishes me the usual happy birthday, and I try to be cheery, but inside I'm screaming. When Mom comes in I make sure she has the correct poster and get the usual hug of gratitude in return. I make sure Kylie has her lunch and her poster, and that we get to the bus on time.

When the doors of the bus open I hurry on before Kylie, refusing to look up at the driver. He'll just remind me that the one person we need to find has disappeared. Kylie's poster bumps me in the back, and I stop walking and turn around. This time I see her expression when her eyes land on Dustin and Alyssa. Her eyes sort of freeze, and then she squeezes past me to join her best friend, Jen. She immediately starts laughing at something Jen says, but this time I can tell the laugh is forced. In her haste she dropped her poster, and I push it into the empty row behind the driver. It's not until I throw myself into the seat that I look up and see the back of the driver's head. I'd recognize that white hair anywhere. I run around the seat to face her.

"You!" I yell. A hush falls over the front of the bus. "You have a lot of explaining to do!"

"Please sit while the bus is in motion," she says sweetly, not even turning to look at me.

"But you ... and then ... but. . ." I know I'm not making any sense.

"Please sit while the bus is in motion," she repeats, firmer this time.

My mouth opens and then shuts again.

"Sit down, Amanda!" Kylie shouts. "You're going to get hurt!"

With a last glare at Angelina, I turn around and hold on to the back of the seat for balance. I sit down as the bus pulls up to Ruby's stop. I force myself to ask her if she needs help with her duffel. She declines, as I knew she would. "You're gonna do great today!" I assure her as she pushes by me.

Might as well tell her this now, since there's no way I'm trying out again. What's the point?

When Stephanie gets on I move closer to the window and slide down so she doesn't see me. If she doesn't see me, I won't have to explain why I'm not getting off the bus when it arrives at school. I stay low and face the window until the bus empties. Even Kylie walks right by me. When I watch her go down the stairs, I remember I had stashed her poster under the seat. I reach down and grab it. But she's already gone. Looking around I see the LEGO kid, Jonathan, heading down the aisle. "Here," I say, thrusting it at him. "It's my sister, Kylie's. If you give it to her she'll be really grateful."

His surprise turns to understanding. "Thanks!" He hurries out of the bus, the poster clutched tightly in his hand.

When the last person exits, I get up and walk to the top of the stairs. Leo is standing there, looking around for me. I call out to him, and wave him on to the bus. He hurries up the stairs and trips when he recognizes Angelina. He barely misses hitting his chin on the step. Once he scrambles to his feet, she presses the button to close the door.

"Please sit while the bus is in motion," she says.

"But you owe us—" Leo begins.

I pull him down into the aisle seat across from me. "Trust me, she won't talk while she's driving."

Angelina parks the bus at the edge of the parking lot and turns off the engine. "Come," she says, opening the door. "Let's go for a walk."

At a loss for words, we obediently follow her to one of the picnic tables where the eighth graders have lunch on nice days.

She sits across from us and folds her hands on the table. She looks thoughtful, but doesn't speak.

"You owe us an explanation," Leo says firmly. "You knew a lot more than you told us."

Calmly she replies, "One might argue that you knew more than I did. After all, you had the benefit of reading Leonard Fitzpatrick's diary."

"How did you know that?" Leo sputters.

"For one, you left the back window open—"

"I knew it!" I mutter.

"And then there were the footprints on the couches from your little celebration."

"Oh, sorry," Leo says sincerely. "But why didn't you tell us about the diary before?"

"I was not aware of its existence," she replies. "So you haven't read it?" I ask.

"Oh, no, I have," she says. "Once I found the loose drawer, I was able to find the diary. I had not known until then how the enchantment played itself out. Alexander Smithy's journal had proved less than accurate."

"Yeah, about that," Leo says, "why did you bother to steal it when you work there? Couldn't you just have read it, you know, on your lunch break?"

"That would have been difficult," she says matter-of-factly, "since I don't actually work there."

"You *don't*?" we exclaim together.

"I don't drive your bus, either," she admits.

My jaw falls open. "What?"

"We have a lot more important things to worry about," Angelina insists gently. "Let us get back to the subject at hand."

With effort, I swallow all my questions and say, "OK so you read Leonard's diary. Now you know the enchantment was real and you know how our great-great- grandparents broke free of it."

"Oh, but they did not break free of it," she says. "And you are living proof of that."

"But they did," I argue. "They stopped Harvest Day from repeating."

She shakes her head. "But that was not the point. When I cast the enchantment, it was to —"

Leo and I jump up from the table so fast we fall backwards over the picnic bench and wind up in a heap on the ground. "What?" we yell as we scramble back on to the bench. "*You* cast the enchantment? How is that possible?" Off in the background the bell rings for first period but I barely notice.

She pulls her thin sweater tightly around herself. "My family has a lot of, shall we say, *longevity* in it. We tend to stick around a while."

"So *you* started all this?" I can't believe it.

"Hadn't mentioned that before, eh?"

"Probably slipped your mind with all the other things you left out," Leo snaps.

"Now, now, young man, there's no need to get hostile."

Leo jumps up again. "Hostile? *Hostile?* We've been trapped in the same day over and over again, because of YOU, and you don't expect us to be *hostile?*"

I pull Leo back down on to the bench. "Shhh, let her talk."

Leo crosses his arms, but shuts up.

"Don't you think I feel bad about what's happening to you? I do, truly. That's why I'm here today. I thought by now the enchantment would have ended and I would not have to get involved. It is never a good idea for the enchanter to entangle herself in her enchantment. Very messy." She gives a big sigh. "I best start at the beginning. The enchantment was for Rex and Leonard to end their feud and to become friends. I gave them a period of one year – no more – and when they couldn't solve their differences during that time, well, time simply halted until they could figure out a way to be friends."

"Which they did," Leo points out, "by being good neighbours and helping the town."

"Yes and no," Angelina says. "All they needed to do was to become friends. The fact that they helped others in the process, well, that was its own reward. All they needed to do was end their day with a toast to their friendship. That's what worked."

"I offered to carry Ruby's duffel for no reason?" I blurt out.

"Nothing nice you ever do for anyone is for no reason. Didn't helping the others feel good?"

I watch the duck wiggle on Angelina's cheek as

I consider her question. It *did* feel good to help my family and Bee Boy. I open my mouth to speak, but she holds up a finger and says, "Let me finish. Your great-great-grandfathers' lives returned to normal, but the enchantment still lay upon them. If ever they fought for a year's time again, they'd wind up in the same position, as would any of their descendants still living in Willow Falls. Amanda, when your family moved back here for your birth, the enchantment started all over again."

"OK," I jump in, "as crazy as all that sounds, I think I understand. But Leo and I made up days ago, and last night we toasted our friendship just like you said."

"Yeah," agrees Leo. "So why is it still our birthday?"

Angelina shifts a bit in her seat. "Well, I'm not sure, to be honest with you. I thought having your party together last night would have done it. I was so certain. I tried to protect you years ago so this wouldn't happen."

Leo frowns. "How did you try to protect us?"

She looks from one of us to the other, then asks, "Do you recall a time before your fifth birthday, you two stopped talking for a few weeks?"

We both shake our heads.

"No? Well, there was some hopscotch incident on the playground, and you didn't speak after that."

"I don't play hopscotch," Leo is quick to assure us. "Anyway," Angelina continues, "I realized back then that if you actually stayed mad at each other for a year, you would have found yourselves in this situation before you were six years old! Imagine going through this at that age."

I shiver involuntarily at that thought.

"After a few weeks, you made up, but it was a close call. So I got to work on a plan that I thought would keep the enchantment at bay, at least until you were out of high school." She sighs again and shakes her head sadly. "But I obviously failed, because here you are."

"I don't understand," I tell her. "What was your plan?"

"It was those little plants you made at the pottery store for your fifth birthday."

My heart skips a beat.

Angelina continues. "I gave Amanda an apple seed from Leo's great-great-grandfather's tree, and Leo one from Amanda's great-great-grandfather's tree. As long as you kept them close, they should have protected you."

242

"But my plant is still growing fine," Leo says. "They're about a foot tall, right, Amanda?"

I don't answer.

Leo waves his hand in front of my face. "Amanda? Tell her how good those plants are. Maybe all we need to do is water them or something and we can end this."

I want to climb under the table and hide. "Um, well, mine isn't doing so good right now."

"What do you mean?" he asks.

"Um, I sort of threw it out the window last year after our fight and it broke."

Leo gapes at me. Angelina exhales loudly. "Interesting," she says, tilting her head. "Very interesting. I should have considered that prospect."

Leo groans and rests his head in his hands.

"I'm afraid now that adding the apple seed enchantment might have made things worse," Angelina says. "Everything might hinge on that, and now, well, it seems we're in a bit of a pickle."

The three of us sit there like that for a while. Leo with his head in his hands, Angelina looking sad and regretful, and me picking at a piece of loose brown paint on the picnic table. I break the silence. "If it matters, the flowerpot could still be down there. No one ever goes into those bushes."

Leo pops his head up and looks at Angelina hopefully. She shrugs. "It's worth a try." She stands up and heads back to the bus. We hurry after her. "Take your things," she says, pointing to our backpacks. "We'll meet again at five p.m., outside Amanda's window."

"What do we do until then?" Leo asks, slinging his backpack over his shoulder.

"Do what comes naturally," she says, then starts the bus and pulls away.

I face Leo. "What does that mean?"

He shakes his head. "Maybe it means we shouldn't worry about the enchantment, and just do what we'd normally do."

"I don't know what that is any more."

"Me neither," he says as we run up the front steps. "And I'm not looking forward to walking into first period a half an hour late."

But when we turn the doorknob to our history class, Ms Gottlieb is still writing on the board. We've only missed a minute of class. With a confused glance at each other, we hurry to our seats just as she turns around. The class groans when they read the words, POP QUIZ.

Maybe Angelina isn't so bad after all. That woman has some skills.

For the rest of the morning I think about her suggestion to do what comes naturally, and about how this whole experience has changed me. On my first eleventh birthday I still felt bad for the crying Bee Boy, but would I have gone so far as to draw up a periodic table for him? I doubt it. Even though I know now that it's not going to help me break the enchantment, I get my hall pass at lunch and present him with his science project. This one wasn't one of my better efforts since I only had a few minutes to do it, but he takes it anyway. After school I pass Leo coming out of the guidance office. But this time that kid Vinnie is with him, and they're laughing! Whatever he did this time must have worked.

At the end of the hall I stop. In one direction is the gymnastics tryouts. In the other is the marching band auditions. I tell myself, *Do what comes naturally*. What would I have done if all this hadn't happened? I make my choice.

Chapter Twenty-Three

As I push open the door to the auditorium, the swell of music fills my ears. I smile. If all of this hadn't happened, I would be trying out for the gymnastics team right now. But it did happen. And that's why I'm here.

I give the musical director, Mr Paster, my name and he assigns me a number. I join the others waiting to audition. The candidates fill up the first three rows of seats. Mr Paster introduces himself to those of us who are new and tells us the results will be posted on Monday. Monday seems like an impossible dream. Will I ever see a Monday again?

It takes a while to get to my turn, and I enjoy listening to the others play their instruments. When my name is called I stand up a bit unsteadily and take the drumsticks that the kid before me thrusts into my hands. I roll them between my fingers as I swing the strap of the snare drum over my neck. I've never played a drum that wasn't attached to a set before, and doubt floods through me.

"Please begin," Mr Paster says.

I nervously straighten the sheet music that is attached to the drum by a little metal stand. Then I close my eyes and pretend I'm back in the basement of that music store, just me, Leo, and the Larrys. I hear the sharp snaps of the drumsticks as they land on the surface of the drum and my feet itch to move. I can see why this is the drum for marching. I refrain from marching across the stage, though, and instead open my eyes and focus on following along with the sheet music. When I finish the last bar I'm almost sad to stop.

"Thank you, Amanda," Mr Paster says, making a mark in his notebook. I reluctantly hand the sticks over to the next person. I glance at my watch. Stephanie's mom should be here right about now. If I miss my ride home, I'm going to be late meeting Angelina and Leo. I run by the gym door just as Stephanie and Ruby emerge from it, sweaty and excited.

"Amanda!" Stephanie shouts when she sees me. "Where were you? You missed the tryouts!"

"No, I didn't," I reply. "I just tried out for the marching band instead."

Her eyes grow wide. "You did?"

Ruby laughs. "Good choice!"

Stephanie steps in front of her to block her from me. "It's not going to be as much fun being on the team without you."

"So you made it?" I ask, trying to act as surprised as I can after doing this so many times.

She nods and can't help the grin spreading across her face. Ruby pops up with, "I made it, too!"

"I knew you would," I reply. "You're really good."

Ruby doesn't answer right away, as though she's waiting for the punch line. But I just smile. She gives me a tentative smile in return.

Stephanie's mom drops me off with about ten minutes to spare. I tiptoe past Dad asleep on the couch, and leave my bag by the stairs so he'll know I'm home if he wakes up before I'm back. I don't want him to worry about not being able to find me ever again.

I slip out the back door as quietly as I can and

run around to the side of the house. Angelina and Leo are already there. Leo is holding up two halves of my broken alarm clock. "Tough morning, eh?"

"Oops, let me take that," I say, turning slightly red. Angelina is on her hands and knees, digging through the overgrowth. She's not afraid to get dirty, that one.

"How were tryouts?" Leo asks as we wait for Angelina to resurface. "Make the team again?"

I shake my head. "But I might have made the marching band."

He grins. "Good job!"

"Thanks. I mean, for getting me to play the other day, it really—"

"You're welcome."

"Got it!" Angelina crawls back out and holds up a big mound of dirt with a foot-tall plant sticking out of it. "This thing is hardy! It fell out of the pot when you threw it, but it took root in the soil. All we have to do is re-pot it and you two should be on your way to Saturday!"

"Will they ever grow apples?" Leo asks.

She shakes her head. "But that doesn't mean it's not an apple tree."

"Does it have to be a real pot?" I ask, concerned that we don't have one.

She shakes her head again. "As long as it's big enough to support it." She places the plant in my cupped hands. "Try not to throw anything else out the window, OK, dear?"

"So what happens now?" Leo asks.

"You celebrate your birthday, you make your toast, and we cross our fingers."

"Will we see you again?" I ask, trying not to let too much loose soil slip between my fingers.

"Probably," she says, wiping the dirt off her hands with a handkerchief. "Can't seem to get out of Willow Falls no matter how hard I try."

Leo and I exchange puzzled looks. Without as much as a wave goodbye, she hurries off down the street.

"Wait!" Leo calls out. "What if it doesn't work?"

But Angelina doesn't turn back. For an old woman, she sure moves fast. We watch as she turns the corner, both of us silent. Holding my hands out in front of me, I slowly move towards the back door. Leo picks up the remains of my alarm clock and follows. "Should I come in?"

I nod and he follows me into the kitchen. "I can't believe it's been over a year since I've been in your house. It looks exactly the same."

"Shh, my dad's sleeping. C'mon." We take the stairs slowly, each creak threatening to wake him. When we get to my room, I motion with my head for Leo to pick up the wicker picnic basket that came with the Dorothy costume. "Guess this thing is coming in handy after all." I gently lay the plant inside and pat down the dirt until it feels pretty firm. "Perfect fit." I pick it up gently and move it to its perch on top of my bookcase, right where the old one used to be.

"I better get home," Leo says. "Any minute Paul the Ball is going to arrive, demanding his dinner. His name isn't even Paul, you know. I guess he just needed something that rhymed with ball."

"Hey, why don't we have our parties together from the beginning?" I suggest. "I can call everyone and tell them not to wear their costumes, and to go straight to your house instead."

"Good idea! I'll tell my mom. After you called this morning she said to tell you she's really excited to see you!"

For some reason the idea of Leo's mom thinking she hasn't seen me in a year is suddenly the most hysterical thing I've ever heard. I start laughing uncontrollably. My side hurts but I can't stop. Leo joins in and we don't stop until my dad walks in, groggy and still wearing his bathrobe and pyjamas.

"Hi, Mr Ellerby!" Leo says, gasping for breath.

"Leo!" Dad exclaims, his eyes bugging out. "This isn't the sight I expected to see when I woke up! I must have been asleep for a long time – when did you two make up?"

I try to stand straight, but my side still aches. "Just today, actually. You know how it is when you share a birthday. Can't hold grudges, right? You don't get any do-overs in life."

"Most of the time," Leo says, still giggling.

I start cracking up again and Dad shakes his head. "I'll leave you two alone to, uh, keep working out your issues."

Before he can close the door all the way, I call out, "Hey, Dad, you don't need to get out your cowboy outfit, the party's at Leo's house now, OK?"

In response, he has a sneezing fit that only makes me and Leo laugh harder.

. . . .

Between me and Mom we're able to reach everyone who had RSVP'd that they were coming to my party. A few people sounded disappointed not to be wearing their costumes, but the mention of cotton-candy machines and a hypnotist helped them get over it. The only place I had to leave a message was at Tracy and Emma's house. They've loyally shown up at my party night after night, never leaving early. I feel bad that I haven't spent much time with them lately. I'll be sure to fix that.

Getting dressed for my party tonight is actually fun for a change. I get to wear whatever I want, and my feet won't hurt. After I wash my face, Kylie comes into the bathroom and offers to straighten the back of my hair when she's done with hers.

"No thanks, I have a thing about having scalding-hot objects too close to my head."

"Are you sure? Your hair kinda poofs up in the back, and well, all over."

"I'm sure." I watch as she expertly makes her straight hair even straighter. Usually she's a bit pale before my party. But this time her face is bright. "You're in a good mood," I note, drying my face with a hand towel. "Did something happen today?"

She smiles. "If you must know, I got a date for the dance."

"But isn't Dustin going with Alyssa?"

She waves her hand in the air. "Who cares? I'm going with Jonathan."

"The LEGO kid?" I slap my hand over my mouth as soon as it comes out.

She lays down the curling iron on the counter. "LEGOs can be a very creative hobby. All the famous architects made their first buildings out of LEGOs."

"Wow, I didn't know that," I say as sincerely as possible. She nods. "Yup, it's true."

"That's cool then, about Jonathan. He's nice." I quickly add, "But not too nice." I once overheard Kylie and Jen talking about boys and they said that being too nice is worse than being a jerk, which doesn't make any sense, but supposedly it will when I'm a teenager.

At a little before seven Kylie and I are climbing into the back of Mom's car when Mrs Becker pulls up to the kerb. Tracy and Emma get out in their full-on Oompa-Loompa costumes. Green hair, orange skin and everything.

"Uh-oh," Kylie says. "You're in trouble!"

I meet the twins halfway up the driveway. "Didn't you get my message?"

They shake their heads. "Why aren't you wearing your costume?" Emma asks.

I shift my weight from foot to foot. "Um, the party's been moved to Leo's house. I left a message a few hours ago. . ."

"Mom always forgets to check the voice mail," Tracy groans.

"So what are we going to do?" asks Emma. "We can't go like this."

I consider the problem. It was one thing when a bunch of us showed up in costume yesterday, but it would be really weird if just two people did. My clothes would be too small for them, though.

"C'mon," Kylie says, surprising me. "Let's go up to my room. I'm sure we can find something."

I smile gratefully and Kylie ushers them off. I take this time to fish my mom's cell phone out of her pocketbook and hide it in the kitchen drawer. Fifteen minutes later they're back outside, wearing Kylie's clothes. Only a slight hint of orange remains on their skin. Their hair is still green, though.

"It wouldn't wash out," Emma says when she sees me looking at it.

"It looks very *mod*," Mom says, getting into the driver's seat. The four of us squeeze into the back while Dad gets in the passenger seat.

"Mod?" I repeat, sharing a smile with the twins.

"Goth? Emo? Punk? I don't know what you kids call things these days."

"You can just say it looks cool, Mom."

"You know what looks cool?" she asks as she backs up into the street. "My Cruella de Vil costume that is currently hanging in my closet!"

I laugh. "Sorry. You can wear it around the house if it makes you feel better."

"I just might."

When we arrive, everything is just as it was last night, but this time we get to watch the hypnotist. He's wearing the same light blue suit he wore at the car dealership, except now he added a top hat. Leo's mom is motioning for everyone to sit on the dance floor in a semi-circle around him. When she sees me and my parents, she runs over and shrieks. All three of us get swallowed up in her hug. "SO wonderful to see you all! Come, come, let's watch the show. We'll have plenty of time to catch up later." She ushers us over and sits me down next to Leo, who is happily munching on a snow cone.

The hypnotist's voice booms across the yard, much deeper than I remember. "I'd like everyone to close their eyes and clasp their hands together on their laps." I look pointedly at Leo's snow cone, but he smiles and keeps crunching his ice. I shrug and turn my attention to the hypnotist.

"Press your hands together as tight as you can," he commands. "I'm going to count down from ten to one and when I get to one, you won't be able to unclasp them."

The audience chuckles. He begins his countdown and when he gets to the end and tells us to open our hands, I expect mine to easily pull apart. But they don't! I pull and pull, but they won't come apart. My eyes fly open. Half the group's hands are stuck, too. Murmurs of surprise fill the yard.

"All right," he says, holding up his hands for order. "Close your eyes again. This time I'm going to count to three. When I get to three, you'll be able to separate your hands." He counts to three, and I pull. This time I'm able to do it. I open my eyes again, slightly freaked out.

"Now, everyone who couldn't pull their hands apart I'd like you to come up on stage."

So that was a test to see who was the most likely to be hypnotized! As kids make their way up, Leo puts his hand firmly on my arm and shakes his head. "Don't go. The first night it was ME that clucked like a chicken!"

"No way!" When I stop laughing, I say, "Don't worry, I'm not going up there. What if he hypnotized me into forgetting we need to make a toast tonight? Then I'd be responsible for messing this up AGAIN. No thanks!"

Leo stands and motions for me to follow. We sneak out of the show and go around to the side of the house where it's quiet. "It wasn't your fault before," he says. "How were you supposed to know that plant wasn't just a plant? My mom's almost thrown that thing out twenty times. You know how she feels – living things are supposed to be outside."

"So why do you still have it?"

He fiddles with what's left of his melting snow cone. "Same reason you threw yours out the window when you were mad at me, I guess. It just reminded me of our friendship."

To break the awkward moment, I suggest, "You should write a poem about all this."

"Maybe I will," he says, tossing his soggy paper cone into the nearby trash can. "C'mon, let's go do our toast now while everyone's out here."

On the way through the yard, we pass two boys who I recognize from marching band auditions this afternoon. One played the cymbals and the other the French horn. When they see me, the cymbals player says, "Hey, you were really good today."

"Really?" I haven't thought too much about the auditions. For one, they might not mean anything if tomorrow never comes, and two, I might have been awful.

Both boys nod. "We need a good drummer for next year."

"Thanks," I say, beaming. "You guys were really good, too."

"C'mon, Little Drummer Girl," Leo says, dragging me inside. We pass on the lemonade this time, and both reach for the iced tea.

"To friendship, forgiveness and tiny apple trees!" Leo says, holding up his cup.

I tap my cup hard against his, almost sloshing the iced tea over the edge. We both drink and grab our throats.

"Ack!" Leo chokes. "Bitter!"

I cough. "Your mom really has something against sugar!"

We force ourselves to finish the cups, not

willing to take any chances. Even though this version of our birthday has been one of the best, I'm SO ready for it to be over.

As we place our cups down on the counter, both sets of parents walk in, talking and laughing. "So," my dad says, clasping us both on the back. "When are we going to hear about how you two made up?"

Leo and I turn and grin at each other. I can feel my own eyes twinkle as we happily shout, "Tomorrow!"

Chapter Twenty-Four

I wake up to a white-haired woman shaking me. "Wake up," she says. "You're going to sleep the whole day away!"

I rub my eyes, but they're still bleary from sleeping and I can't focus them. Why is Angelina in my bedroom? This can't be good. Replanting the tree must not have worked. My stomach sinks.

"Seriously, Amanda, it's almost ten o'clock! Don't you want to go to Leo's and open your gifts?"

Her words clear the cobwebs from my brain. I see now that only half her head is white, the other is black. The voice was Mom's, not Angelina's! I quickly assess the situation. It's light in my room, which means it's way past the time my alarm usually goes off. Mom is here, wearing her Cruella de Vil costume instead of her business suit. The middle of my room is empty of any and all balloon figures. This can only mean one thing. It's SATURDAY!!! I throw off the covers and almost knock Mom over.

"It's so good to see you!" I tell her. "Even looking like that!"

She laughs. "It was your idea. Might as well get some use out of it before I have to return it to the costume shop. I laid out yours, too. I bet you'd look adorable in it."

I follow where she's pointing and shudder when I see the all-too-familiar Dorothy costume on my dresser. "No thanks!"

"Suit yourself. I'd like you to get up soon, though. The Fitzpatricks are expecting us for brunch." She turns to leave, then stops. "By the way, did you put my cell phone in the kitchen drawer?"

"Um, I don't remember?"

She looks doubtful, but doesn't press it. "When I found it this morning, there were quite a few messages on it."

I don't say anything.

"One in particular was quite distressing.

Seems that I lost my job. Fired after ten years of dedicated service."

"Wow, Mom, I'm really sorry. Are you OK?" She's handling it much better this time than all the other times, but I'm not sure why.

She nods. "Surprisingly, I'm OK What you said yesterday was very wise. I do have other dreams. I've always wanted to be an interior designer. I could work out of the house so I'd be around more. Maybe this is just what I needed to get moving on that." She looks across my room and frowns. "In fact, I can start my new job right now. That plant is awfully scraggly." She heads over to it and starts to lift up the basket. "Why don't we plant it outside. I'll get you a nice small fern for your bookshelf."

"No!" I say too loudly.

Startled, she lets go of the basket and it falls back on to the shelf. "Whoa, OK, sorry. I didn't know you were so attached to it." She peers closer. "Is that the same plant you used to have?"

I nod, holding my breath that she won't notice that instead of the hand-made pot, it's planted in the wicker basket that's supposed to be returned to the costume shop.

"Odd," she says. "I don't remember seeing it in

here for a long time." Then she shrugs it off. "Downstairs, half an hour."

Once I'm alone, I steady the plant on the shelf and then do a little dance around my room. It's Saturday! It won't be my birthday again for a whole year! What an amazing feeling! Before I go downstairs I wrench open my piggy bank and pull out some bills. I need to make a stop on the way to Leo's house.

All our presents are piled on the hall table when we walk into the Fitzpatricks' house. It's a tradition that we open them together, which probably explains why I was never in any rush to open mine all week.

When Leo comes into the room he says, "Is it OK if I steal Amanda for a few minutes? I want to give her my gift in private."

Our parents wave us away, too busy gushing to each other over what a fun party it was last night. We hurry down the hall to Leo's room. I stop at the doorway. I haven't been in his room since our tenth birthday. Leo walks right in, oblivious to my hesitation. I take a deep breath and follow him. His room looks different. The wallpaper with the race cars on it is gone, replaced with light brown paint. Instead of his floor being covered with pieces of toy dinosaurs, I only see two, and those are on shelves. His apple tree plant is front and centre on his desk, still in its original pot with his little purple handprint on it from when we were five.

Leo clears his throat to get my attention. With his hands behind his back, he says, "This gift serves two purposes. First, it's something you need, and second, it will remind you of our adventure." Very dramatically, he presents me with a gift bag like he's serving it on a platter. It's small, no bigger than a lunch box, but heavy.

I reach in and pull out an alarm clock. A bright yellow SpongeBob SquarePants alarm clock! I start laughing. "Where did you find this?"

"My mom took me to the mall this morning. I remembered seeing it in the window of the toy store when we were there."

"It's great, thank you!"

"Aw, it was nothing," he says, trying to be modest.

I reach into my back pocket and pull out a brown bag wrapped with a rubber band. "I have something for you, too."

He snatches it from my hand and eagerly pulls

the bag open. "Postcards?" he asks, holding up the contents in his hand.

I nod. "They're for later, when we're grown up. To make sure we're never out of touch, we can just mail each other these postcards every six months. That way a year will never go by."

Leo looks confused. "But aren't the little apple trees supposed to protect us from it happening again?"

I shake my head. "Only until we're eighteen, remember? We're going to need to keep in touch till we're really old, or else we'll be stuck in the same day again."

"Would that be so bad? To have a day out of time again?"

I stare at him. "Really? Are you serious?"

"Sure! This time we'd know all the rules, and we'd know how to break out of it."

Imagine doing this on purpose! It's almost unthinkable! Then again . . . it's not like we asked for this enchantment in the first place. And there were some really great parts.

"We wouldn't do it any time soon," Leo insists, his eyes shining. "Since we'd have to stop talking for a year before. But maybe like, twenty years from now or something."

"OK," I announce. "Twenty years from now. It's a date."

"It's a date," Leo repeats, and we shake on it.

Leo's mother sticks her head in the door. "You guys are much too young to be dating!"

"MOM!" Leo cries, turning bright red.

Mrs Fitzpatrick puts her arm around me and leads us out of the room. "Of course, when you ARE old enough, I'd love it to be you." She squeezes my shoulder.

From behind us Leo groans. I just laugh. And outside the window, an old woman with a birthmark in the shape of a duck, looks on and smiles.

About the Author

Wendy Mass is the author of the award-winning books for young readers *A Mango-Shaped Space*, *Leap Day*, *Jeremy Fink and the Meaning of Life*, *Heaven Looks a Lot Like the Mall*, *Every Soul a Star*, and *11 Birthdays*.

She lives with her family in New Jersey. Visit her online at www.wendymass.com.